GAPTOWN LAW

GAPTOWN LAW

LOUIS TRIMBLE

THORNDIKE
CHIVERS

This Large Print edition is published by Thorndike Press, Waterville, Maine, USA and by BBC Audiobooks Ltd, Bath, England.
Thorndike Press, a part of Gale, Cengage Learning.

The text of this Large Print edition is unabridged.
Other aspects of the book may vary from the original edition.
Set in 16 pt. Plantin.

LIBRARY OF CONGRESS CATALOGING-IN-PUBLICATION DATA

Trimble, Louis, 1917–
    Gaptown law / by Louis Trimble. — Large print ed.
        p. cm. — (Thorndike Press large print western)
    ISBN-13: 978-1-4104-2956-8
    ISBN-10: 1-4104-2956-3
    1. Large type books. I. Title.
PS3539.R565T75 2010
813'.54—dc22   2010020049

BRITISH LIBRARY CATALOGUING-IN-PUBLICATION DATA AVAILABLE
Published in 2010 in the U.S. by arrangement with Golden West Literary Agency.
Published in 2011 in the U.K. by arrangement with Golden West Literary Agency.

U.K. Hardcover: 978 1 408 49281 9 (Chivers Large Print)
U.K. Softcover: 978 1 408 49282 6 (Camden Large Print)

Printed in the United States of America
1 2 3 4 5 6 7 14 13 12 11 10

GAPTOWN LAW

CHAPTER ONE

The stage from Walla Walla made an overnight stop at The Falls before going on east. Matt Ross left it at the hotel, getting his war bag out of the rear boot and taking it inside the two-story log building. He was headed north and east where no stages ran.

He nodded pleasantly to the hotel clerk and laid out a silver dollar for his room. The man raised the coin and let it drop on the board counter. His expression showed that his action was habit rather than any distrust of Matt Ross.

"Going north tomorrow, Matt?"

"When Jeremy Cotter gets here," Matt said. He leaned against the counter, showing hunger for familiar conversation on his long homely face. "He should be along with the freight later tonight."

The clerk bobbed his head in agreement. "It ain't safe to travel up alone," he commented.

"Not yet," Matt said. He knew what was coming, and even though time had cooled his feelings he didn't enjoy hearing it.

The clerk spun the silver dollar and caught it before it fell over. "They ever find out who got your pa?"

"Not yet," Matt said again. He waited a moment, but the clerk was silent. Matt moved his big body easily, straightening from the rough counter and taking a sack of tobacco from his pocket. He rolled a cigarette carefully, not wasting much tobacco, using slow deliberate motions of his long broad fingers. He licked the cigarette and put it between his lips. Leaning forward, he took a light from the clerk.

"I heard you sold your pa's freight line to Jeremy Cotter and Sam Garton."

"Yes," Matt said.

"Thought maybe you'd keep it and try to get the ones who ——"

Matt leaned forward and blew out the match still burning between the man's fingers. "You hear a lot down here," he remarked. His smile took the edge off his words. "You think a lot, too."

The clerk was looking at the burned match head. "Some say Jake Dill done it. Some say Cole Pitman." He raised his eyes expectantly to Matt's face.

"People talk too much," Matt said. "It's up to the law to handle it. If I went out and shot up Dill or Cole Pitman, I'd be breaking the law, too. Even if one of them did it."

"A killing over six months old and —" The clerk broke off and gave Matt a sour grin. "Law? Who's the law in Gaptown?"

Matt stepped back, his smile friendly. "I am," he said. "I am, now." He laughed and walked out the door, turning toward a saloon down the street. He knew a few of the people walking by, and he nodded briefly as he passed.

His smile faded as he stepped into the cool dimness of the saloon. He was no pretender, but he had found that showing his true feelings about his father's death only kept the talk going longer. He and Tim Ross had been close, and Tim's death had brought a cold violent anger that time had turned to hard ice but had not diminished.

Not wanting to think of it, he shook his head and moved into the saloon. He sat at a table, enjoying the feeling, after the stage ride, of being again on something that held still. He bought a glass of whiskey and a cigar and leaned back, relaxing in the coolness. It was early, not dark yet, and the saloon was nearly empty of customers. He could enjoy watching them without having to look at too much at once.

So he noticed the dandified young man that came in shortly, wearing fine polished boots, gray trousers, a pearl-gray cutaway with a white linen shirt, and a high stock. He wore a matching gray top hat and carried a pair of gloves in one hand. Someone at the bar whistled. Matt smiled because the man seemed totally unaware that his costume was out of place.

He spoke to the bartender and then turned, crossing the empty dance floor toward Matt. He stopped by the table, making no move to sit down but standing in an easy posture.

"Ross?" His voice was resonant and friendly. He was darkly handsome, with an open face and smile and a thick dark mustache.

Matt said, "Yes. Sit down." He liked the lack of both subservience and arrogance in the young man.

"Adam Bede," the stranger said, sitting. His smile broadened into a rich chuckle. He laid his hat and gloves on the table top. "It's a poor joke that's one-sided."

"I read the name," Matt said, "in a book. If that's what you mean."

Adam Bede's thick eyebrows rose and met in surprise. "Even up here ——"

"I like a man to say something when he talks," Matt said.

"I will, then," Adam Bede agreed. "The inn-keeper directed me to you, thinking you might be able to find transportation for two to Gaptown. A lady and myself."

"I'm going up with the freighters," Matt said. "In the saddle. There's always room for more, and wagon enough for your baggage. But it's no trip for a lady."

"A singularly self-possessed lady," Bede said.

"She's welcome," Matt answered, "but warn her. I ride with the freight train because there's safety in numbers. But that doesn't always hold." There had been no safety for Tim Ross last spring, not even when surrounded by an alert crew.

"It's a raw country, then?" Adam Bede asked. "I heard it was."

"It won't be," Matt Ross told him. "Not for long. But it is now." He looked into the grave eyes of the man opposite him. "The freighters will be in tonight and out early in the morning."

Adam Bede rose, picking up his hat and gloves. "I'll tell the lady." He offered Matt a quick bow. "But she's very determined, so the warning is wasted."

Matt merely nodded and watched Adam

11

Bede move away. He and a lady going to Gaptown with winter coming on. It was an unusual happening, unusual enough to wonder about.

He drank his whiskey and smoked his cigar, puffing leisurely. He was still thinking about the man and woman as he took out the letter he had received at Walla Walla and smoothed it on the table top. He had to bend forward to make out the handwriting.

My dear Matt: As soon as you get that shipment bought and on its way to me you are fired. I got no money to pay a helper now that I got to pay my share in hiring a sheriff.

The sheriff is you, voted in four to two at yesterday's town meeting. Ezra Meecham and Sam Garton were against, claiming you are too young and might be against some people because Cole Pitman or Jake Dill is supposed to have shot your pa.

But we decided you were the one who hollered loudest for law and so should be given a chance at the job. And I made them see you are a fair man and not as young as you sometimes look to be.

The pay is one hundred gold which is the same as Cole Pitman pays his gun hands he calls cowboys. I expect you will earn it.

Cole Pitman took Lucy Morgan out last week right after his men had a wrangle with Morgan's Double M. Most of the windows on lower Main Street were shot up, so come home quick. There's a dance Saturday.

Your salary also includes one meal a day at Daisy's place and half the board of your horse from Luther Colban. Ezra is all for changing the name of Gaptown right off so if we ever get to be a state we can form a county and be a county seat. But I say let's clean up the town first or there won't be enough folks left to make a county. So come on home.

Your friend and one-time boss,
Abe Parkis

Matt folded the letter slowly and put it away. Old Abe wasn't as funny as he sometimes liked to think. But the way he put things didn't matter. Here was Gaptown buying itself some law and trying to stop helling, and that did matter.

In a way it bothered Matt, being hired as sheriff. He had been away when Tim was ambushed and shot and had not found out about it for a month. But on his return he had started talking up law, something unorganized Gaptown had never had, and finally it seemed that they had come to his way of thinking. He would have preferred another man for the job, because he knew that his father's death was still fresh in the minds of most of the town. But having talked for law, he could hardly turn it down when the chance came.

Picking up his whiskey glass, he drank the remainder of the contents quickly. He felt impatient to get back to Gaptown. The feeling took the pleasant edge off the relaxation he had been enjoying, and he wished he hadn't reread the letter. He got up and walked into the new darkness, smelling the dust on the sharp dry fall air. He threw his cigar into the street and turned in at the hotel.

Taking his bag from its place by the counter, he nodded again to the hotel clerk and went on up the stairs. In his room he stripped off his coat and shirt and washed up in cold water. He brushed off his trousers and wiped his boots and returned downstairs.

Sitting at one end of the long table, he ate quickly and silently, since there was no one nearby that he knew and he was usually a restrained man with strangers.

Leaving, he noticed Adam Bede by the door. A tall and arresting woman sat next to him. When he slowed his step to nod at Bede, she studied him coolly and without pretense. Wide gray eyes met his blue ones, holding them until he had gone past. He went quickly, not being easy around women. He felt that his rawboned looseness had none of the grace of the dandified Bede.

Going to the counter, he lounged against it, rolling and shaping his after-supper cigarette. Deliberately, he said to the night clerk, "Who is this Bede?"

"Stranger. Came on yesterday from the East."

When the clerk stopped and waited, Matt said impatiently, "And the woman?"

"A Miss Gail Winter. Stranger, too."

"Both going to Gaptown?"

"So Bede said," the clerk agreed. He nodded and laughed at Matt. "No relation. They seem strangers to each other except for having ridden the stage together." He reached out to straighten the desk pen standing in the bottle of shot beside Matt's arm. "Going to Gaptown is their business."

"And mine," Matt said abruptly. "Now it's mine."

"Then," the clerk said, "ask them." He looked at Matt, still amused. "I don't hear

15

everything down here."

The next morning Matt found Jeremy Cotter ready with the freight outfit. The old man was still sleepy, having come in late the night before after a lead horse had held them up by throwing a shoe a few miles to the south; he was finishing up with the blacksmith when Matt spoke to him.

"If it doesn't mean throwing off Abe Parkis' freight, I've been saying you have room for baggage and a woman."

"The woman can ride on my wagon," Jeremy Cotter said. He was dirty from trail dust but otherwise clean. He had known Matt for the ten years he had freighted for Matt's father. "I smell better'n the others, and she'll get less dirt up front with me."

"You're too anxious," Matt remarked. "You must have seen her."

Jeremy Cotter chuckled and spat tobacco juice against the stained shop wall. "Already promised her a ride. She didn't figure on any man doing her chores."

The blacksmith gave a last touch with his rasp to the shoe, and Jeremy Cotter stooped to squint critically at the job. He nodded in satisfaction and straightened. "We'll pull out in under an hour," he told Matt.

Returning to the hotel, Matt changed to

16

his work trousers and range boots, heavy shirt and cowhide vest. Since it was a gray day with a hope of rain in the flat clouds, he carried his slicker out and tied it behind his saddle.

His horse acted ready for the three-day ride, full of vinegar from having been boarded in the month Matt had been gone. He was a deep-chested sorrel gelding, big and sturdy and quick to answer Matt's touch.

Adam Bede, on a rented horse and still in his finery, looked odd set against the rough dusty trail and the rough dusty men who rode it. The woman sat in comparative comfort on Jeremy Cotter's wagon. She wore green, a full-flowing tight-waisted gown with a matching jacket and an ornate but small hat that covered very little of her rich blonde hair. She looked, Matt thought, as if she would have better sense than to dress like that.

Occasionally he was alongside the lead wagon where he could see and admire her profile, not missing her firm finely drawn chin. She kept her eyes straight ahead, talking to no one but Jeremy Cotter, and to him very little. None of the country along the way — stretches of open pine, mixed with prairie, and then thick forest with trees

17

standing bole to bole and choked with buck-brush and serviceberry and small seedlings stunted from lack of sunlight — seemed to catch her interest. When they had crossed the cable ferry and were winding along the broad river, blue and then green, now and then catching the reflection of dark firs or lacy tamaracks turning golden under the fall frosts, she glanced but once and then returned to her silent straight-ahead staring.

To Matt she looked as Adam Bede had said, a determined woman. Her purpose lay ahead in Gaptown, and this rugged country rimmed by rough-edged mountains could not distract her. She was young, he judged — perhaps his own twenty-four, perhaps less — and she rode with the untiring ease of youth, letting the steady jolting run through her body without resistance.

Adam Bede took it differently. He could not seem to get himself settled comfortably in the stock saddle, and by the end of the first day he found it hard to get down from his horse. They bedded on dry ground above a slow-moving stream, and the next morning Matt had to help him into the saddle.

The second day was a slow twisting trip over a low pass that carried them east and then north again. Adam Bede kept his light smile, but Matt could see that it was an effort for him.

"Does this go on forever?" he asked once, riding up beside Matt.

"You may wish it would," Matt answered, "if they try to attack the train."

"Who is *they*?"

Matt had been smiling, but the smile left him. "We aren't sure," he said. He studied Adam Bede's dark features broodingly. "We have no proof." He rode away, thinking of that and of his new job that lay just ahead.

It would come tomorrow if it came at all, in the last narrow valley before they reached Gaptown. The men were riding easily now, but tomorrow they would sit with their guns handy across their knees and their heads moving sharply to study each shadow in the heavy forest.

It angered Matt to think that a freight outfit would need an armed guard when it was a bare two-hour ride from the town itself. And it angered him that the men responsible could run free because there was no law to ride against them.

Matt was in the lead when the freight train topped the last low rise before Gaptown. Ahead lay the narrow flat valley. Matt reined up and studied the country carefully. Eastward, to his right, the land sloped upward and then leveled to a flat sparsely timbered bench before it became a series of steep ragged hills. From the rise where he sat, Matt could see the cluster of log buildings that marked Cole Pitman's Bar Cross.

A creek, low after the dry summer, twisted and turned below him. Following its course with his eyes, he could see some of Morgan's beef pastured along its banks. The valley held by Morgan's Double M was patched with prairie, where the creek did not reach, and heavily timbered where the channel widened to form a swamp. The Morgan ranch was out of sight behind a shoulder of the west mountains. The buildings were set on high ground, so that they stayed dry during the heavy spring runoff that often caused the creek to fill up the valley.

Matt drew alongside Jeremy Cotter as the first freight wagon came abreast of him. The old man pulled the horses to a halt and glanced over at Matt.

"Looks peaceable," he said, through the cloud of fine dust settling around them.

The woman, Gail Winter, still looked straight ahead, her expression impassive. Matt said to Jeremy Cotter, "Maybe the law scared them off."

The old man laughed at Matt's dry tone. "More likely," he said, "they're waiting to see what you'll do." He spat tobacco juice into the deep road dust. "Or they're too busy finishing fall roundup."

Matt looked quietly down at him. "That's no way to talk, Jeremy. You sound as if you were accusing someone."

Jeremy Cotter turned his head and squinted at Cole Pitman's benchland. "Just idle talk," he said, and lifted the reins.

Matt watched him progress down the easy grade to the valley floor. Adam Bede was riding alongside the second wagon, and Matt called to him.

"Stay close from here on in," he warned.

Adam Bede brushed futilely at the dust coating his fancy trousers and nodded. Matt remained where he was until all six wagons had passed and dipped downward. He waited a few moments more, until the train had become a long snakelike line of dust spurts ahead of him.

To his right, a trail angled upward. It ran along the western edge of the bench, dropping down near the town. It was this trail that Tim Ross had chosen last spring for his first trip in. Going out, he had used the valley floor, since although the snows were gone frost still remained in the ground and kept the trail hard. On his return, he had taken the freight over the higher ground to avoid the water and mud made by the springtime wildness of the creek.

Matt looked at the trail somberly, remembering what the freighters had told him. There had been no attempt to rob the train that day. There was nothing more than the crack of a single rifle, and Tim Ross had pitched from his seat and fallen beneath the wagon wheels as the startled horses lunged forward. . . .

Matt spoke softly to his horse, and the big sorrel loped toward the dust cloud marking the freight train. They could do that to him, too, he thought. It was easy enough for a man in the forest to drop a rider on the open trail. It would be an easy way to get rid of the threat of law.

But more likely Jeremy Cotter was right. They would wait to see what Matt would do. Or, he thought, they would wait to see if he was worth being afraid of.

Chapter Two

A half hour from town, Matt walked his horse beside Jeremy Cotter's lead wagon. "You called it," Matt said.

Jeremy Cotter nodded and spat into the dust spurting from the wagon wheels. "They're waiting to judge you," he answered. His dust-reddened eyes twinkled a little. "So ride ahead and let 'em get started."

Matt tipped his hat to Gail Winter and spurred out. He rode at an easy lope to the top of the sloping grade that dropped to town and walked the sorrel the rest of the way. Main Street started at the foot of the hill and ran north two short blocks before a wall of rock halted it abruptly.

The south end was where Matt expected most of his trouble. Next to the abandoned Chinese laundry to his left was Bill Lamont's big saloon. Opposite Lamont's was the smaller saloon, Hewitt's, and on the corner, going north, Lippy Hollister's hotel. The street that crossed Main was Hill, so called because it met steep slopes at either end of its two-and-a-half-block length.

From Hill Street north Matt expected less trouble. Abe Parkis' general store and post office was opposite the hotel, across Hill, and the other stores fronted on Main, all north of Hill, so that the town was cut in two, with the day life above and the night life below. State, running parallel to Main and along the east slope, was a street of homes where all those with money or position lived. An alley ran between it and Main, but it was clean and not like the alley behind Lamont's saloon where the town's roustabouts lived.

That was all there could be to Gaptown. The hills hemmed it in, preventing further growth. It was just a gap that let the freight trains to the British Columbia mines find their way through the jumbled low mountains up to the border. Those mountains were an effective barrier, with the freight highway snaking west and north again down a canyon that was the only outlet. Just south of the border, a wide cup in the hills held the last freight stop, the few buildings there having been dubbed Shackville by the freighters.

South there were only the two cattle ranches, Morgan's and Pitman's, while in the mountains north and on either side of town a few miners worked scanty gold and silver claims. When they had money they boasted that they had hit a rich pocket, but mostly it was profit from driving the ranchers' beef to the Canadian mines.

Matt remembered Gaptown when it was merely Abe Parkis' original tiny store that served Morgan's ranch and the early prospectors. The town had grown only after the coming of Tim Ross and his freight outfit.

After Tim Ross had established himself, others followed quickly. Sam Garton showed up to run the freight office and to look hopefully for the coming of stages; Luther Colban, the blacksmith, opened a livery stable; Ira Morris came with his hardware store; and Ezra Meecham arrived with a sawmill, setting it on the creek at the west end of Hill, and stayed to become a banker and think of money instead of trees. The saloons, Lamont's and Hewitt's, had come early, and Bee Clancy, about whom few spoke openly, a little later. At the crest of the boom, the businessmen had formed a committee and built a log jail and a small log building they called the city offices. People laughed at these, just as they laughed at the pretension of naming streets which were no more than dusty dirt tracks or mudholes, depending on the season.

Matt had laughed, too, but now he was glad for the city office and the jail building. He knew the people, their temperaments and faults, and he expected trouble with winter coming on. There was trouble in anything that was bottled up too tightly.

Abe Parkis was standing on the board sidewalk in front of his store, and Matt

25

threw up a hand in a wave as he passed by. He took his horse to Luther Colban's livery stable, easing out of the saddle gratefully after the long ride. Luther Colban came over, moving his big body in a studied slouch.

"Howdy, Sheriff." He was a bull of a man with a bull's voice to fit his body. "Freight coming in?"

"Hour or so," Matt said. "Sheriff — that sounds funny."

"You'll get used to it," Luther Colban said.

Matt nodded and turned away, walking jerkily until he loosened up. He passed Ezra Meecham's bank and cut across the street to where Abe Parkis stood. He was a lean wrinkled old man, barely up to Matt's shoulder, and he stepped back to be able to look more easily into Matt's face.

"I fixed the city office and the jail up for you," he said, without preamble. "I expect they'll get some use now."

"I don't plan to change much," Matt said. "Not for a while. People have to get used to me, Abe."

"Outside of Ezra Meecham and Sam Garton they'll go along," Abe Parkis said. His voice was rusty, like a hinge needing oil.

"I expect trouble from Ezra," Matt admitted.

26

"Ezra is always out for money," Abe said. "Since he handles all the business for the saloons, he wants 'em to sell more so he can make more. Don't go at him too hard at first. His mind is yellow like gold and it clinks when he thinks. That's Ezra's way."

Matt brushed aside Abe's humor with a movement of his hand. "What the law is to one man it has to be to all of them."

Abe said slyly, "There are some here who think paying for a sheriff is a waste of money. They say that if things get too bad people will get together and make their own justice."

Matt answered sharply, "Justice? Justice without law behind it is more lawlessness." It was the basis of Matt's belief, and he expounded it, not noticing the pleased amusement on Abe's wrinkled face.

"It's as if I hunted down and shot the man who killed my father," Matt said. "I may think Jake Dill did it, so I kill him. His son Toby shoots me, and then you, as my friend, shoot Toby. That puts your life in danger because one of Toby's friends may shoot you to get even.

"What I want, Abe, is to build up respect for the law. Let the people realize that there is law — and that it's here to protect them, not hurt them. Law like that stops crime, prevents it. It could have saved my father."

"You can't build up that kind of law without fear," Abe said, no longer smiling, "and that means force."

"If I use their kind of force, I'm no different from them," Matt said. "I'll try my way."

Abe shook his head. "Sometimes you need a club to make men admit that the law works for them as well as against them. You'll have to fight Gaptown with its own weapons, Matt."

"I'll try my way," Matt repeated stubbornly.

Abe dropped the subject. Instead, he said, "Ezra Meecham and Sam Garton figure you'll side with Dave Morgan over Cole Pitman."

"I never liked Cole since he came," Matt answered, "but it won't stop me from trying to see his side."

"I told 'em that," Abe said. "Even though he ain't got a side, you're the kind to try and make one for him." He looked up and down the street and gave his sour grin. "Seems peaceful now, but wait until Saturday night."

"It's too close," Matt said, "to give me more than time to plan what I'm going to do."

"While you're figuring," Abe remarked,

"you better see Lamont and Bee Clancy and them kind."

"I'll do that," Matt said uneasily.

Abe sensed the uneasiness. "You got to learn that there's all kinds of people, even in Gaptown. And they all handle different. You got to learn never to trust folks too far and not to get too friendly with them. Get too friendly, and you might as well give up."

"In that case," Matt said pleasantly, "I'll be leaving. I talk to you too much as it is."

Abe Parkis laughed and watched Matt stride in his deliberate steady way around the corner and down Hill Street. He went to State, turning north and going to where his own house stood. It had three rooms, built by his father. It had been lived in enough so that the inside was settled into comfort to fit Matt just as it had fit Tim and him before.

Matt knew that the town had thought about his home when they elected him at meeting. He owned it, and he didn't eat too much, and he usually took one drink a day and sometimes forgot that. He was steady and had worked for Abe Parkis winters and rode the range for Dave Morgan summers during his growing up. Since then he had been buyer for Abe in connection with the freight trains, so he knew both the ranchers' and the businessmen's points of view. And as he had sold the freight outfit to Jeremy Cotter and Sam Garton after Tim's funeral, he had no ax to grind beyond finding his father's killer.

Sam Garton, Matt was sure, would come around soon in agreeing that they needed law in Gaptown. He wasn't so sure of Ezra Meecham. Ezra, having gold where his brains should have been, was constantly afraid that the Gaptown saloon and gambling business would go to Shackville, the freight stop a day's pull to the north.

But he wasn't going to worry about Ezra until the time came for it. It wasn't his way to take up a thing until he was faced with it.

He changed his dusty trail clothes, washed up from the long ride, and lay on his bed, resting a little. Then it was time to get up and meet the freight, get his bag, and see that the newcomers were taken care of. Matt had no intention of being a welcoming committee, but he wondered whether Bede and the woman would go north or south on Main Street.

He left his house and angled onto Main by way of the alley and the city office. There was a side door facing the alley, and Matt found it unlocked.

Inside, behind a peeled log railing that cut the room in two, was a homemade desk, and near it were two ancient chairs. Matt saw a shined-up star lying on the desk top, and he pinned it on his cowhide vest. He felt self-conscious about it, but he knew that it was something he would have to get used to, so he went out through the front door to Main Street.

The freight outfit was already in, having swung along the north side of Sam Garton's. A small crowd had gathered, and everyone was watching Adam Bede and Gail Winter as they went into Garton's office. Matt reached the edge of the crowd and pushed his way through.

A rough voice drawled, "Howdy, Sheriff," and, glancing up, Matt saw the unshaven face of Jake Dill. He nodded coolly and pushed on. Behind him, he heard Jake Dill say, "Guess Matt don't remember people now he's got that star on his chest."

Matt turned, looking down on the man. "I remember you well enough, Dill." His voice was low, not carrying far. He moved on again, conscious of Jake Dill's mocking half-toothed grin.

Inside the station, Sam Garton stood talking to Adam Bede and Gail Winter. Garton saw Matt looking thoughtfully at the

31

woman, and his massive stomach quivered with amusement. He was a thick man, thick from front to back and from side to side. Some said in the head as well, but Matt knew that there was a shrewdness in his pale blue eyes that was worth respecting. Garton was red-faced and bald-headed, given to laughing until he shook but seldom letting the amusement show on his features.

"Matt," he said, "I want you to meet these people."

Matt took off his hat. "We met," he said briefly. Bede was studying the star on his vest. "You staying at the hotel?" Matt asked.

"Whichever hostelry is the finest," Adam Bede said, in his sonorous voice.

"There's only the one," Matt told him. He glanced at the woman. "Lippy Hollister isn't much for caring for ladies."

"Mrs. Cowley'll take care of you," Sam Garton told her. "She runs the boarding-house." His belly quivered with some inner amusement. "You show her there, Matt. There's a rough element in this town, ma'am." When Matt reddened in spite of himself, Garton added, "Of course, Matt's only been on the job less'n an hour, so he ain't had quite time enough to run the roughs out of town. Have you, Matt?"

Matt forgot his embarrassment and looked

with amusement at Garton. Now that he was being made the butt of a private joke, he felt more at ease. "Seems to me, Sam, you didn't want any sheriff at all."

"I voted against him," Garton said, unabashed. "A young man ain't usually a steady man."

Gail Winter's rich voice interceded for Matt. "The sheriff looks quite steady to me."

"We shall see," Adam Bede said. "If Gaptown is half as bad as one hears — we shall see."

"You've been talking to the freighters," Matt said to him. "Some think it's a quiet enough place." He ended further conversation by moving toward the door.

"I'll have your baggage sent, Miss Winter," Sam Garton called.

Nodding her thanks, Gail Winter caught up with Matt. He held the door for her and followed her onto the sidewalk. The crowd had thinned, but there were enough remaining to make him acutely conscious of the situation, especially when she put her hand on his arm and walked silently down the sidewalk with him.

"Being sheriff's got its advantages," Jake Dill's voice boomed out suddenly. "Maybe I'll get me a star."

Matt stiffened and half turned. Gail

Winter's fingers put pressure on his arm. "No, please."

He twisted his head, looking quizzically down at her. "Why?"

She kept her face straight ahead so that he could see only her determined profile. "You don't know anything about me, Sheriff."

"Any woman —" He realized that he still didn't know to which end of Main Street she belonged. "Any woman," he said, more forcibly. They walked on, saying nothing.

She was the first to speak again. "It's a bigger place than I expected."

"It's as big as it can get unless we spill up the hillsides," Matt answered. They came to the bank. "We cross here. Watch the dust. It's bad for this time of year."

He took her arm beneath her elbow, helping her through the powdery dust. They reached Abe Parkis' store and stopped. Abe was leaning his withered body against the door frame, surveying them. He tipped his eyeshade to the woman. Matt introduced her.

"Howdy," Abe said. She nodded, smiling very slightly.

"Taking her to Mrs. Cowley's," Matt said.

"Good place," Abe said. He studied her shrewdly, and then he nodded them on.

Matt led her along Hill to State. On the corner, Mrs. Cowley's sprawled over a good deal of land. The house was a two-story affair of rough lumber, with thin battens over the cracks between the boards.

Inside the front room, Matt turned her over to the sharp-faced proprietress. He stood, turning his hat in his hands.

"If there's anything I can do to help ——"

Her gray eyes smiled fleetingly at his halting words. "Thank you," she said, in her low voice.

Matt backed hastily out. Once around the corner, he walked more slowly, musing. A mighty pretty woman, he thought. Full face she was even nicer than profile. A little tall, but nice.

Abe Parkis had him by the shoulder before he realized he was back at the general store. "Find out why she's here, Matt?"

"No."

"You should," Abe said. "Maybe she belongs at Bee Clancy's instead of Mrs. Cowley's."

Matt gaped a little. "Now, Abe, that's no way to talk."

Abe Parkis snorted. "Maybe Sam Garton was right. You're a mite young."

"Maybe," Matt agreed. "But that's no way to talk about a lady."

Abe squinted up at Matt. "Find out if she's a lady before you go calling her one."

"I'd rather call her a lady and be wrong," Matt said, "than chance calling her something else and be wrong that way."

"A woman coming here alone with winter just ahead and her not knowing anyone —" Abe broke off and went on into his store, and Matt stood where he was, wondering how much of it was advice from Abe and how much was a try at showing him the meaning of his new job.

He saw the dandified Adam Bede starting across the street, up by Luther Colban's, and went that way. When he noticed Jake Dill mounting a horse beyond the freight station, he hurried his step. He knew Jake Dill well enough to guess what would happen.

Adam Bede had reached the center of the street when Dill came level with him, swinging the horse as close as he could without knocking the young man down. The cloud of dust the horse raised obscured everything but the sound of a voice raised in violence.

Before the dust had fully settled, Matt was striding into the center of it. Things were easily visible by the time he reached the riderless horse. Jake Dill sat spraddle-legged in the dirt, and Adam Bede was standing, wiping his hands on a white linen handkerchief.

Dill was cursing as he rolled to his feet and reached for the gun hanging on his hip. Matt stepped in, knocked Dill's arm in the air, clamped onto his wrist, and turned. Dill let go of the gun, and Matt took it with his free hand.

"You letting strangers haul people off their horses, Sheriff?" Dill's face was wrathful beneath ragged whiskers. "You're too full of oats."

Matt broke Dill's gun and dropped the shells into his own hand. "I know that trick, Jake. Next time you get rough I'll lock you up. That's the law." He thrust the empty gun forward. "Now ride out of here."

Jake Dill took the gun and jammed it into his holster. He stared angrily and open-mouthed at Matt. "Law? What law?"

"My law," Matt said quietly. "My first law. Get, Jake."

"Your law?" Dill saw a small crowd lining the sidewalk. "Hear that? Matt Ross's law!"

"Gaptown law," Matt said. He turned his back to Jake Dill and glanced at Adam Bede, who was standing aside, dusting himself with flicks of his handkerchief and smiling a little.

"Better get to the hotel," Matt told him.

"Like Sam Garton said, the town isn't cleaned up yet."

"I'm beginning to think it soon will be," Bede said, with quiet respect. "Allow me to buy you a drink, sir."

"On duty," Matt said briefly. "But I'll walk with you."

Bede glanced back to where Jake Dill still stood in the center of the street. "His mistake was in reaching too far," Bede said. "He almost invited me to take hold of his arm."

Matt said, "Next time he'll use his gun. Jake's that kind."

"I'll remember," Bede said. He glanced around the small town. Quite a different companion from Gail Winter, he was talkative and inquiring, wanting to know the name of every store, its owner, and any problems a new citizen might face.

"Then you plan to stay?"

Adam Bede glanced up at the mountains. "I like it here," he said. "I see no reason why I should not stay."

Matt slowed his step. Reared in the West, he had grown up believing that a man's business was his own until offered. But as sheriff he felt a responsibility to ask questions.

38

"What's your business?" he demanded bluntly.

"I'm a newspaperman, sir. A journalist," Adam Bede stated. "I see no paper. I see no printing establishment at all."

"We send our printing to the coast or to Walla Walla," Matt said. "Only we don't have much." He tilted his hat, scratching at his red hair with his thumb. "Outside of Ezra Meecham's bank and some printing for Abe Parkis, we don't have any."

"Ah! Well, until a demand is created I see that I must fall back on a more profitable if more dubious profession."

It took Matt a moment to untangle it. He said, "You're a gambler, then?"

"A dealer, sir. I excel in the honest deal."

Matt stepped to the street to make the crossing at Hill. "That'll be something new for Gaptown. You'd better see Bill Lamont. His is the biggest saloon — across the street there."

"Thank you," Adam Bede said courteously. They went into the small dark lobby of Lippy Hollister's hotel. Lippy was at the desk, a crude affair across one corner of the room. He looked up sourly as they approached.

He was a dour man of indeterminate age, graying whiskers and a bald head making him seem older than his body appeared. He was slender and wiry and reputedly the strongest man in town, regardless of size. He spoke as if conserving his strength for some contest.

"A room, sir," Adam Bede said. "The finest room."

"All alike," Lippy told him. "Bed and dresser and chair. No bugs. Dollar a night if you got your own blankets."

"If I haven't?"

"Sleep 'thout 'em," Lippy said indifferently.

"I have some extras," Matt said. He was amused at Adam Bede's expression. "This is Gaptown."

"Thank you," Bede said. He turned to Lippy. "My baggage is on the way. Have it sent up, will you?"

"Be down here when you want it," Lippy said. "Dollar in advance."

Adam Bede raised his finely drawn eyebrows, shrugged, and paid with a gold coin. He received the change, thrust it into his pocket without counting it, and waited.

Matt grinned. "No key. Go up and try the rooms. The first empty one is yours."

"Amazing," Adam Bede said. He looked around a little more, smiled at Matt, and then went quickly up the rough stairs.

CHAPTER THREE

Saturday arrived, as Matt had feared, too quickly. He was not prepared, and he knew that if trouble was to come from either of the ranchers it would almost surely come tonight. This was the Saturday of the monthly dance — probably the last dance until spring, if the hint of winter in the air held any meaning.

Finishing his meal at Daisy's, Matt started down Main Street. It was already well past dark, and both Pitman's and Morgan's crews should be in town by now. Matt made an automatic check of the door at Ezra Meecham's little bank and then, continuing down the same side of Main, went into Bill Lamont's.

It was a big place with a dance floor between the long bar on one side and the tables on the other. At the rear was the gambling layout. For all that Gaptown catered to a handful of miners and freighters and there were only the two cattle ranches to provide steady customers, a game or two always seemed to be going on at Lamont's. Tonight, Matt noticed that the faro and poker tables were crowded, and there was even a group at the roulette wheel, though it was early for it.

41

At the bar, he spotted a half dozen of Cole Pitman's men and, farther down the line, two men who rode for Morgan's Double M. Neither Cole nor his foreman, Texas Zinker, was in sight, nor was Dave Morgan, who had taken over the Double M since age had crippled his father, old Pete. Matt nodded to those he knew and spoke to the bartender.

"Cole upstairs with Lamont?"

"Ain't seen him."

"Figuring on arresting him, Sheriff?" one of Pitman's men asked. He and his friends guffawed.

Matt turned. "Not until he does something to be arrested for," he said equably.

The men guffawed again. "When'll that be?" the speaker wanted to know.

"Not long, I expect," Matt said, and went out.

Across the street, at Hewitt's he found Jake Dill with some of the crew from his mine up in the hills. Dill was already half liquored and on his way to find a fight. Matt said, "Take it easy, Jake."

Dill was a squat heavy man who always looked as if he needed a shave. He showed Matt a gap-toothed grin. "Figure on seeing that I do, Sheriff?"

"I'm just telling you," Matt said. He

turned away. Dill knew what he meant; a Saturday night seldom went by without a brawl being started or finished by Jake and some of his men.

"He must think that star's heap big medicine," Dill said mockingly.

Matt went on, realizing the pointlessness of words, and knowing that Jake Dill was one of those he would have to watch more than closely.

By eight o'clock he was at the community hall back of the old parsonage. The two-piece orchestra was already tuning up when he arrived, and a fair crowd of early comers was on hand. There was no sign of either Gail Winter or Adam Bede. Over to one side, Matt saw Dave Morgan talking to Luther Colban's daughter. He walked their way and spoke pleasantly.

Dave Morgan smiled, his young rugged features showing nothing but friendliness. "Evening, Sheriff. Looking for Lucy?"

"Never saw her miss a dance yet," Matt said.

Dave Morgan shook his head. "I think you lost your girl, Matt. Cole Pitman had the nerve to come calling — and he's bringing her to the dance."

"Fine," Matt said honestly. "Maybe you and Cole can keep away from each other's

43

throats now."

Dave Morgan's expression showed what he thought of Matt's words. "Fine!" He showed the lack of tolerance of the stubborn man. "If that fool sister of mine weren't twenty years old I'd turn her over my knee." He started to add more and then stiffened in such a manner that Matt turned to see where he was looking. Luther Colban's daughter murmured something and walked away.

Cole Pitman was coming in the door. With him was his long loose-jointed foreman, Texas Zinker. Between them was Lucy Morgan.

Matt turned to Dave Morgan. "Take it easy," he cautioned.

Morgan looked at him almost with contempt. "Your girl walking with the man who killed your dad, and you tell me to take it easy!"

"In the first place," Matt said levelly, "Lucy never was my girl. We just grew up together, that's all. Her mind is her own; her choice of men is her own. In the second," he went on, "we can't prove that Cole shot my father. Shooting Cole isn't the lawful way."

"You can get proof of it," Morgan said flatly.

44

"I'd still want due process of law," Matt answered.

Morgan made a disgusted sound deep in his throat. Before he could form it into words, Pitman, with Lucy and Zinker, came up to them.

Cole Pitman was a big fine-set man, young enough to have his full strength but old enough to have judgment. His hair was graying at the temples, and that gave a look of steadiness to the rough impatience all of his judgment could sometimes not hide.

"Evening, Matt — Sheriff."

Matt nodded and spoke to Lucy. She was small and dark and probably the prettiest girl north of Spokane Falls, and she had a quick smile for Matt as she welcomed him back. Frowning at her brother, she turned to Cole in such a way that there was no doubt as to who her escort was.

Dave Morgan shifted his weight and said, "I was just saying, Cole, that Matt ought to get proof you shot his father."

His voice was loud, carrying above the scratchy tuning of the fiddle and the dulcimer across the way. Cole Pitman reddened, as everyone in the hall stopped talking and turned to look toward the little group. Pitman put out a hand, touching Texas Zinker, who had stiffened like a stretched wire.

45

"That's enough of that," Matt said sharply. "Both of you can leave your feuds outside of town."

"As I intend to do," Pitman said, in an easy voice.

There was a rustling from the orchestra, and a tune came quickly, stridently, breaking the deepening silence over the room. A few couples moved to form a dance.

Lucy turned toward Pitman. "Shall we dance, Cole?" With her hand on his arm, they moved away. Matt could hear, ". . . sorry for my brother ——"

Dave Morgan scowled. Matt said, "Don't be a fool, Dave. Cole has three men to your one."

"And half our land," Morgan pointed out, "and he's aiming to get the rest of it."

"For the first," Matt said, "that was free land he took. Your Double M was just making use of it — and without cattle enough to need it. For the second, I haven't seen any signs of Pitman moving in on you."

"Then you're going to be one hell of a sheriff," Morgan answered, and moved abruptly away.

Matt went slowly out, feeling tension as he went through the room. He continued to feel it, still building, as he made his way back to Main for a second check of the saloons. When David Morgan was in such a mood as this, almost anything could happen. And Matt knew Cole Pitman well enough not to be fooled by his affable manner; neither he nor Texas Zinker had ever backed down on a fight.

"It's up to me," Matt told himself, and he wondered just where to begin.

Later he saw Dave Morgan at the bar in Lamont's, talking to his men. On what Matt figured to be his final round of a suspiciously quiet Saturday night, he went back to Lamont's and found that there was neither a Double M man there nor any of Pitman's crew.

"The crazy fools," he burst out, and broke for the dance hall at a quick run.

He didn't quite make it. He heard the first shot as he came abreast of the parsonage. A woman screamed, and then the doors of the dance hall burst open, and light and people spilled out. Two more quick shots cracked sharply on the night air, and a man's curses rose above the clatter of people hurrying out of the way.

Matt breasted those coming out, shouldering his way inside just as someone quick-wittedly blew out the last lantern. Darkness closed around, pinpricked only by the glow of a cigar in the face of the fiddler. Another shot blossomed in the room, and the cigar disappeared.

Matt stood spraddle-legged in the doorway, his gun out, his weight settled firmly. "Get a light!" he shouted. "No man goes out of here. Get a light."

There was a hoot of laughter from the other end of the room, but otherwise no sound. Finally, after what seemed endless hours to Matt, firm footsteps slipped along the wall. There was the flare of a match. Someone cursed, and a gun went off. Evidently the arm of the man shooting was struck, for the bullet plowed into the floor with a harsh splintering sound. Framed in the match glow was Lucy Morgan.

She lighted a lantern and then walked quickly along the wall, lighting others as she went. Matt said, "Thank you, Lucy."

There was light enough to see now. The room was emptied but for a dozen men. Lined up on one side were Cole Pitman, Texas Zinker, and six of their hands. On the other was Dave Morgan with three men. One of them was on the floor, and a thin trickle of blood ran from his side to the scuffed boards.

Matt's usually drawling voice was harsh and clipped. "No man moves," he ordered. Holding his gun in plain sight, he walked across the room and looked down at the wounded Double M man, then up at Dave Morgan.

"What started this?"

Cole Pitman came walking insolently across the room. Matt put out a hand, curbing Morgan's sharp movement. "It's hard to say how these things start, Sheriff," Pitman said smoothly. "The first thing I knew two of the boys were shooting at each other."

Matt looked again at Morgan. "Your version?"

Morgan's tight-pressed lips opened slightly. "That's the way of it," he said.

Matt felt hopelessness flood him. Neither man would give him any satisfaction; he should have known it before he asked. They had deliberately built up this fight, and to both the law was the enemy of the moment.

Matt said, "Get some help for your man, Dave." His voice rose. "And all of you ride out. Cole, take your crew first."

"And let them ambush us?" Morgan demanded.

Matt was tempted to say, You let your crew get drunk and then called them in. That's your look-out. But, aloud, he said, "You're each responsible for your crews. Any man hurt, and I'll see that one of you goes to jail and stands trial for murder."

"Can you make that stick, Sheriff?" Pitman said softly.

Matt stared coldly at him. "Sooner or later — yes."

Pitman turned to his crew. "All right, boys, time to ride."

But as they went out the door, Matt heard Zinker laugh and say, "Oh, well, this isn't the only Saturday night in the world."

Before Matt went wearily to bed that night, Abe Parkis and three others cornered him. "You let it get away from you," Abe accused.

"So I did," Matt said.

"You'll have to put some teeth in your law, Matt. They're all laughing at you."

"I'm bound to step on someone's toes," Matt said. "I can't satisfy everyone."

"Then step," Abe said. "Step and be damned. You're the sheriff. You going to let them ride you down?"

"What if it happens to be your toes?"

"I'll still be back of you; so will every man with any sense. Step ahead, Matt."

Matt looked at the others. They nodded. Luther Colban said, "We're backing you."

"Remember that," Matt said. "Just remember that."

A single light glowed from an upper back

window of Bill Lamont's long after the rest of Gaptown was dark. The light came from a hanging lamp in the sitting room reserved for Cole Pitman. He and Texas Zinker were there alone.

Zinker was hungrily wolfing a thick beef sandwich; Pitman contented himself with a glass of beer that he sipped slowly. He watched his lanky foreman chew and swallow, bite out a great chunk of bread and meat, chew and swallow again. Zinker's loose brown beard moved in rhythm with his long jaw. He was, Pitman thought, a crude man in some ways, but it was not an offensive crudeness. It wouldn't have mattered if it had been offensive. Pitman knew that Zinker was a man he could not get along without.

Finally Pitman said, "This range isn't big enough for two, Texas. We can't expand beyond what we have now."

"True, Captain," Zinker agreed, in his studied voice. "But this is no time to change things. Tonight was a mistake."

"That was Morgan's doing."

"You shouldered him into it," Zinker said, "because you wanted to test the new law."

Pitman lit a cigar and waved it impatiently. "Control the town and you control the range. Ross is no different from his father.

51

He forces a man to go against him."

"Beating him down won't be hard to do." Zinker knew his boss, just as he knew that his own usefulness was not that of a foreman — any competent cowhand could do that kind of work — but of a balance wheel. Without thinking it through, he recognized the fact that he had devoted himself to keeping Cole Pitman's impatience from tearing down his plans. And so he said, "Come the right time, it can be done." He was drinking a glass of whiskey as a chaser for his sandwich, and he emptied the glass before raising his eyes to Cole Pitman.

"You're a frightened fool!"

"And you an impatient one," Zinker said equably. "Winter is coming on. There's not much a man can do here in the winter."

"We didn't stop fighting battles in the Civil War because of winter."

"We'd have won 'em cheaper and easier in the summer."

Pitman waved his cigar again. "I haven't time to wait," he said harshly.

"Then you'll lose all you've gained," Zinker answered. "A man that can't wait is a man that can't win."

Their eyes met and held, and it was Cole Pitman who looked away first, shaking his head in bafflement. "I'll hear you out," he said finally.

"When the snow is gone — then is the time," Zinker said. "A winter of quiet softens people, Captain."

"Go on. Go on."

"I didn't run the Union Army, but I do know that someone planned the campaigns."

He spoke slowly and deliberately, letting his words hit Pitman one by one, heavily, so as to break through the barrier of his impatience and hold him.

"You know these things better than I do, Captain; an army takes time to get organized. First, it's got to know what it's going to fight. Then it figures out where the enemy's toughest point is. And it tries to see if it can't weaken that point — maybe cut it down from behind."

"Go on," Pitman said again, but this time more calmly.

"I hear from one of the men that Dill wants to prod the new sheriff."

Pitman nodded. "Ross can be the tough point," he agreed.

"Don't let Dill loose yet," Zinker advised. "The time isn't ready. And he's more impatient than you, Captain." He settled back, his say finished. His job was to cool Pitman so that the man's mind would begin to work. Zinker had never found himself capable of finishing a plan, only of creating its beginnings and then carrying through what his captain worked out.

Pitman took his time, finishing his beer slowly and puffing leisurely on his cigar. Finally he said, "Winter can make a man soft; it can also give him time to prepare his defenses. But no army can build a good fort if it's being sniped at all the time."

"Ah," Zinker said. He hadn't thought it through this far.

"So," Pitman went on, "I won't turn Dill loose, but I won't hold him back, either. Let him and his men keep the sheriff moving. Come spring, we'll see how much strength Ross has had time to build for himself."

Zinker nodded. "What about Morgan?"

Pitman smiled. "The same for Morgan, Texas. The lower his spring count after roundup, the less strength he'll have."

Zinker said, "Ah," again, and left the table. He stretched out on a settee nearby. Pitman got up and went to the small bedroom off the parlor where they were.

"We ride out early," Pitman said. "Call me at daybreak."

Zinker made a half mocking, half respectful salute. "Yes, sir, Captain, sir." He got up and blew out the lamp, then returned to the settee.

And Gaptown was completely dark and silent — as if it needed rest for the winter shaping up ahead.

CHAPTER FOUR

Matt was awake early Sunday morning, letting his mind work over the problem that had sprung up the night before. He realized that he was being tested — by Dave Morgan as well as by Cole Pitman. *He* realized, too, that even though Dave was his friend, his consideration would be no greater than that of anyone else. Dave thought that the way to right a wrong was by personal retribution — as it had always been done in this country. Matt determined to see both Cole and Dave immediately — to take the test to them instead of letting it be carried to him.

The fall air was too soft to suit Matt as he rode south along the freight road. He had seen these Indian summers before. A long late fall always broke violently into winter. He looked back at the first spiraling morning smoke of Gaptown and thought of it under snow — belly-deep to a horse and more coming down.

It was then that men could do nothing. From the mountains and the ranches they came into town, into Lamont's and Hewitt's, looking for outlets for their bottled energies.

He thought, If I could get them to accept the idea of law before then . . . But already the grass was brown, the ferns curled and sere, the tamaracks pale gold instead of green; and the aspen and birch rustled their dry dying leaves.

He came into sunlight at the top of the hill. Farther along, he angled southward and eastward, up the gentle grade to Pitman's bench. The high mountains behind it cut out the sun, leaving him again in early morning shadow. Once high enough, he could glance across the valley and see signs of the Double M coming to life, the sun on the buildings. That was the way of it. Morgan got the first light, but long after his Double M was softened by shadow the late sun warmed the Bar Cross.

The only sunlight they shared was that of midday, and Matt thought that Pitman would want even that all to himself if there were some way of getting it. He wanted the swampy valley land that stretched from the foot of his bench to the west mountains, and that he had some chance of getting.

The reason was easy enough to see. Pitman's pasture was drying. The bench, well watered only in the spring, could not support the stock Morgan's damper land could manage. Nor was there the native meadow hay to cut for the long winter feeding. It was this need of Pitman's for the land preempted by Morgan, because he had settled first, that had started the tension. It had not been in the open until the recent shooting frays, but Matt knew that these were just a beginning. Cole Pitman was the kind of man who would never rest until his land was the best and his cattle numbered the most.

Matt topped the bench and followed the curving trail along the timbered rim until another smaller trail branched from it. This led east along a creek bed that had been dry since early summer and brought him to the knoll on which Pitman's fine log home stood.

Matt rode to the rear of the house. Men stood around the corrals just beyond, and the smell of morning coffee came from the kitchen. Matt sat his horse, using the time to roll a cigarette, until finally a rear door opened and Cole Pitman stepped into sight.

"Morning, Matt — Sheriff." He sniffed

the early air with the pleasure of a man who appreciated such things. "Come and eat."

Matt stepped from the saddle and looped his reins over the hitch rack. He walked along a board path to the porch. "I ate," he said pleasantly, "but I'll take coffee." They stood facing one another, each man smiling to conceal his dislike.

The dislike had started the first day they met. Matt, long and gawky at nineteen, had served Pitman in Abe's store. He had not liked the newcomer's rough-shod Army arrogance nor his sneering way because Gaptown was too remote to carry all the fine things he wanted to buy. They had never spoken of it but the dislike was there, lying quietly, growing like a mushroom in a damp cave.

Pitman held the door. Inside, Matt followed him through the kitchen to a small room that looked down into the valley. Pitman made no pretense of eating with his men. Matt knew his belief: he was the captain. Texas Zinker, seated in a chair beside the table, raised his small eyes, half obscured behind the brown beard that grew high on his cheeks. He said nothing.

Matt took a chair and looked over the benchland, watching the coming sunlight suck in the shadows. He drank coffee and smoked a cigarette, waiting patiently for Pitman to finish his meal.

When Pitman was through and had lighted a cigar, he said, "Come about last night?"

"No," Matt said. "That's done, Cole." He dropped the squeezed remains of his cigarette and made a second one. Finished, he said, "If it happens this Saturday, I'll do something."

"I thought you'd come with a warning," Pitman said equably.

Texas Zinker spoke for the first time. He had a deep voice, slow so that it sounded reined in but without being too cautious. "Maybe the sheriff's heard rumors that something might happen."

Matt's smile was easy. "I don't go by rumors, Zinker. If I did, I might try to run in the Bar Cross for shooting my father."

Cole Pitman let out a small impatient breath. "No," he said. He took his cigar from his mouth and held it pointed at Matt. "I told Tim to keep his freight wagons off the bench trail in the spring. It's my land, and I don't like it rutted and overrun. I told him, and he came anyway."

"The valley road was deep in mud," Matt said. He was prodding. This was the closest he and Pitman had come to talking about it.

"What does that matter?" Pitman demanded impatiently. "It's my land. I rule it. But I didn't shoot him." He returned the cigar to his mouth and leaned back in his chair.

Matt said, "All right," quietly. He felt the amusement of Texas Zinker's glance and turned to him but he watched both men when he spoke. "I came to tell you about the law. There'll be no guns in Gaptown on Saturday nights."

"That's foolishness," Pitman said harshly.

"And no liquor served to drunk men," Matt added.

"The men," Zinker said, "won't like that. What do they do, Sheriff, sneak into the woods for their drinks?"

"When they've had enough," Matt said, "let them ride home or go sleep it off." Zinker just laughed, and Matt stood up. "I'm going to see there's no more Saturday night fighting, no more windows shot out on Main Street, no more chance for innocent bystanders to get shot."

Pitman merely shrugged, puffing on his cigar as if all this were no concern of his.

Zinker said, "Men get bottled up working.

60

You can't blame them for cutting loose a little."

"They can have their fights out of town — out of my territory," Matt said.

"We'll see — Saturday," Zinker answered.

"It's a warning," Matt said. "You know where the law stands. Check your guns at my office or at the saloons when you ride in."

Cole Pitman showed his impatience. "Law! Let men handle their own quarrels."

"No longer," Matt said. "Gaptown is growing up."

"Sure," Zinker said, and laughed. "Gaptown is growing up and the sheriff, here, is putting long pants on it."

Matt ignored him; he was looking down at Cole Pitman, waiting for further words, wanting to know what he could expect from the Bar Cross on Saturday night.

But Pitman's impatience had disappeared. "We'll see," he said. "We'll wait and see."

Kowing he would get nothing more, Matt left. Outside, he mounted his sorrel and walked the horse back to the trail. The sun covered the bench now, but it was no longer pleasant to see. He had expected opposition and, in Pitman's quiet words, he sensed cold sure strength. Pitman would not bend; he was not a malleable man. He would have to be broken before he would yield.

Matt was sure now of what he had known all along — the Bar Cross would try to ride him down. Not because he was Matt Ross, but for what he represented.

Reaching the valley, Matt crossed the lowlands. The trail ran through small patches of prairie, each fenced off with two strands of wire to keep the stock from drifting into the hay. But the wire was cut now and the gates were down to let the stock onto the stubble, so Matt rode without hindrance to the high spot where the Morgan buildings stood above the spring flood level.

Lucy Morgan came to the veranda as he rode up. She leaned on the railing, smiling a welcome as he removed his hat.

"I thought the sheriff had forgotten his old friends."

Leaning there in the morning sunlight, she was a very pretty girl. Her black hair curled in quick ringlets around her face, giving her an air of vivacity that was matched by her readily smiling mouth.

Matt left the horse, tying him loosely, and mounted the steps. "This is no social call, Lucy."

She held out her hand to him. It was small but hard and strong from handling a rope or the reins of a working cow pony. Until just recently, she had ridden the range with the men. Matt, when he had worked for Morgan, had learned to respect her skill.

"You're welcome, anyway," she said, mocking his seriousness.

Inside the front room it was cool and shadowy except for one splash of sunlight that came in through an east window. Old Pete Morgan sat there, his legs blanket-wrapped, the sun picking out the angry lines of his face.

He was crippled from age and a fall, and his own futility boiled hotly inside him. "If I could get up, I'd whip you, Matt."

"If you could get up," Matt told him, "you'd be doing my job."

Lucy laughed. "He says it isn't a social call, Dad."

Old Pete thrust his head forward so violently that his fine white hair floated upward with the movement. "You came to push your law down our throats?"

Matt knew that the old man could joke, but the Morgans were quick-tempered men, and sometimes their jokes were on the edge of anger. He sat on the settee, his hat over one knee, and shook his head.

"I came to explain it, Pete." Laying aside his hat, he took out a sack of tobacco. "I've been to Pitman's. I explained it to him. There'll be no guns Saturday nights, no liquor to drunks."

The old man laughed raucously. "I can imagine what the men will say — and what Lamont will say. And when you told it to Pitman, he said, 'Yes, Sheriff. Anything you say, Sheriff.' Bah!" He drew a long breath. "You're a fool, Matt. You'll never make it stick."

"So Pitman seems to think," Matt said. "But as long as I'm the sheriff I intend to try." He finished rolling his cigarette and struck a match for it. "If they don't want law they'll have to get rid of me."

There was a moment of silence while Pete Morgan studied him, waiting for him to go on, and Matt sat stiffly, knowing that he could destroy a long friendship by saying the wrong word.

Lucy moved forward in her quick fashion, lifting Matt's hat from his knee. "You'll stay for dinner?"

"No," Matt said, "thanks. I have to get back to my job."

"They're helling in Gaptown," Pete Morgan said. "Matt has to go stop them."

The heavy sarcasm only made Matt smile. He let the old man see his amusement. "They aren't yet, Pete. But they will be. And when they do, I'll stop them."

He stood up, went to the big rock fireplace in the center of the back wall, and tossed his match into it.

"Gaptown is growing, Pete." He was no longer amused. "What happened last night won't happen again. Not while I'm the law. Tell Dave he'll have to see that each man checks his gun somewhere as soon as he rides in."

"You think you'll stop men fighting that way?"

Matt shook his head. "There's no way to stop men fighting, Pete. Half a man's life is made up of fighting. For something or against something ——"

"Or just for the pleasure of it," Lucy put in.

"Then," Matt said, "let them take their pleasure outside of town."

"Pitman won't," Pete Morgan said testily. "Just because you tell him. Pitman's getting proddy, Matt." He leaned forward in his chair. "Does your law say that a man can't defend what is his?"

"The law is there to defend it for him."

"And while the law is getting around to defending it, another man takes it away." Pete Morgan scowled at Matt. "Damn it, I've fought my own battles before. I'll not let any other man fight them for me now."

Matt said again, "Gaptown is growing Pete. When a place grows up it stops brawling like a dirty-faced kid." He saw that his words meant nothing to Pete Morgan. The old man had lived in his own fashion for sixty years, and it would be hard for him to see any other way now.

Throwing his cigarette into the fireplace, Matt walked toward the door. "My hat, Lucy?" She gave it to him and he looked back at Pete Morgan. "Tell Dave," he said.

The old man was silent, but Lucy, following Matt to the veranda, said, "I think it's fine, Matt." She smiled encouragement at him. "Men do too much fighting. Why can't they talk it out instead?"

"Will Cole and your brother talk it out?"

"Dave isn't like Dad. He'll see your meaning."

Matt said bluntly, "Did he see yours when you went out with Cole Pitman?"

She faced him squarely, laughing at him. "The sheriff should learn to step softly." Her black curls danced as she shook her head. "He hasn't seen. Not yet. But he will, Matt."

Matt did not laugh back. "Be careful, Lucy. The man you choose is your affair, but Dave might not think so."

He had to leave it at that. She only smiled and returned to the house. Riding away, he realized that he had got no more satisfaction from her than from her father. And he would get even less from her hot-tempered brother, Dave.

Dissatisfaction worked on him as he returned to town. These men could not see that violence only created violence. His belief in his own way was strong, but already he could feel the cross-currents that threatened to sweep him aside.

It was a helpless sensation, that of striving for balance. No man could change by a word, an order, and yet Matt knew that he could accept nothing less than full compliance. He had meant to move in slowly, to give them time to absorb this thing.

"But it can't be," he said aloud. It was now or not at all. With the town, it was one thing; but with these men, accustomed to the range, to their own solutions of problems, it was another.

And, as before, Matt was sure that Saturday could tell him the answer.

That night, late, making his rounds, Matt slowed when he reached Bee Clancy's. It was an old house, the first two-story place in Gaptown. Ezra Meecham had lived in it when he ran the sawmill only a short distance west across the creek. The growth of Gaptown had moved him onto State, and he had sold to Bee Clancy for a large profit.

Bee's was almost dark, with curtains drawn over all the windows. Matt walked to the front, turned toward the door, hesitated, and then swung away. He went directly to Mrs. Cowley's, across from the church. He had been putting this visit off because it was distasteful to think about, but he knew that putting off distasteful things was something he would have to overcome. He walked deliberately up the steps of the boardinghouse and opened the door. It gave into a good-sized room in which the boarders ate and later sat around to talk or read or just look, depending on the taste of each.

Under a lamp in the far corner Matt saw Gail Winter. Mrs. Cowley came from the kitchen, drying her hands on an apron. She looked inquiringly at Matt. He nodded to her, turning his hat in his hands.

"Callers leave at ten," Mrs. Cowley said in her sharp voice. Her mouth thinned out.

"I'm working," Matt said to her. He smiled pleasantly and crossed the empty room, halting by a vacant chair that was next to Gail Winter. She had a book in her hand and she closed it, placing it face down on her lap and raising her eyes to him. He was impressed again by their clear grayness and by the fine features she had.

"I've been expecting you," she said. "Sit down." Her voice was full and warm.

He sat and, when Mrs. Cowley had returned to the kitchen, said, "I came to see if things are all right."

She smiled, obviously not believing him. "All right, yes. But I want a house to live in. A house of my own."

"There's a vacant one across the street, next to the dressmaker. Ezra Meecham owns it. He owns most of the houses." Seeing her thoughtful look, he added, "He owns almost everything around here."

"I'll see him then, thank you," she said.

Her grave courtesy bothered him, and he sought to pierce it with tact. "Haven't you any friends here?"

"No."

She left her answer at the single word, not following it with the explanation that he wanted. He drew a deep breath. He had to ask, yet he would rather face Cole Pitman and his crew on Main Street than do so.

"Why are you here, then? What are you going to do?"

He sat stiffly. She watched the flush creep up his face as he spoke. She thought, He is

69

not good-looking, and she wondered why that should occur to her. But she saw sincerity in his bony features, and she felt his strength as well.

"That cost you a lot to ask," she said. Her smile relieved some of his embarrassment. "I think I'll teach," she went on. It amused her to see the further relief on his face. A teacher was so completely a respectable person.

"We need a teacher," he said. "There hasn't been one since the minister left town. Maybe you could use the church as he did. Then you could live in the parsonage. I'll ask Abe Parkis."

"Is he your guiding star?"

"Abe is a hand at getting things done." He rose. "I'll say good night, Miss Winter."

"Good night." She extended her hand. He took it, looking down into her eyes. Finding nothing there beyond her words, he turned away, moving two slow steps before he forced himself to look back at her.

"I almost forgot. You didn't say why you came here."

She stood, stepping close to him, touching her tongue to her lips as if they needed moistening. "A letter from a friend," she answered. Her eyes were defiant. "Her address was 'in care of Bee Clancy,' Sheriff."

Matt had known that it would be this way ever since Abe Parkis had spoken to him of Gail Winter. Abe would know because as postmaster he looked over every one of the dozen or so envelopes that came in or went out through his store each month.

Matt said, "I wouldn't mention it. If you want to teach . . . that is, people wouldn't want you on State Street if — if ——"

She laughed, a soft sound without malice. "I think I'll ask you to be my first pupil."

"I've had my schooling."

"Were you given lessons in tact, Mr. Ross?" She went past him and up the stairs. Matt, reddening, walked out, jamming his hat on his head.

Gail Winter continued on up to the tiny room she had been given. It was clean but more comfortable, and the confinement of it irked her. She was used to freedom of movement, and four walls with a sharp-faced guardian below were things that she did not relish.

Raising the shade and the window, she looked down on the nearly silent town. Her room was on the rear corner, so she could see a bit of Main Street as well as most of Hill. Matt had gone on, but presently she heard his footsteps as he came up the alley. He was faintly visible when he turned

71

toward Main alongside Abe Parkis' store. She recognized him by his long deliberate stride, and she did not move aside until his footfalls were beyond hearing.

She thought again of what he had said and how he had said it. She smiled a little as she lighted the lamp. He had not meant to hurt her with his bluntness but had been offering a kindness.

She thought, too, of her retort to him. She said aloud, softly, "Maybe I could stand schooling in tact myself."

Chapter Five

Matt spent the middle of the week familiarizing himself with the eccentricities of each of the buildings he checked on his rounds. The owners of some disdained to lock their doors; others had locks for which Matt had to have extra keys made. He fretted at these time-consuming small points, but he did not neglect them since they were all parts of his work.

First, however, he made sure that all those concerned knew of his first laws. He started with the hotel. Lippy Hollister was behind his desk, chewing tobacco meditatively. Matt went straight to the point.

"There'll be no more guns carried in town

72

on Saturday nights, Lippy. They all have to be checked here or in the saloons or at my office. Tell your roomers."

Lippy rubbed his chin, making a rasping sound. "You're moving fast, Matt."

"Do you think we'll get law and order standing still?"

"Lots of men are naked 'thout their guns, especially on Saturday."

Matt turned away. "It'll save your front windows, Lippy. Pass the word."

He was next door to Hewitt's saloon, and he went in there. It was a mean one-roomed affair with only two tables for gambling and no dance floor. The bar occupied so much of the space that there was scarcely room between it and the far wall for a man to pass out without having to curl up as he fell.

Three men were standing at the bar, and Hewitt was behind it. Matt motioned to him. "Come out back," Hewitt said.

He was tall and amply mustached, and wore what Matt believed to be the dirtiest apron between Fort Snelling and Seattle. In the tiny rear storeroom, he leaned against the wall, rolled a cigar around in his mouth, and waited.

"We've got a few laws now," Matt said. He started to shape a cigarette. Hewitt was not much of a power in Gaptown, but Matt

73

wanted to keep the slight friendliness that there had always been between them. He repeated what he had told Lippy.

Hewitt said briefly, "That's good — no guns."

"And no liquor to a drunk," Matt continued. "You can sell enough without serving drunks."

"You trying to ruin a man's business?"

"No," Matt said patiently, "I'm trying to save him his business." After Hewitt's skeptical snort, he added, "They want to make this town a good one. If we get to be a county seat someday there'll be a lot of trade."

Hewitt spat the end of his cigar on the board floor. "Women and preachers," he said sourly. "The hell with it."

Matt finished rolling his cigarette, put it in his mouth, and snapped a match alight on his thumbnail. "It's the law, Hewitt. Try it for a while before you cry."

Hewitt straightened from the wall. "What else can I do? I ain't big enough to fight you." He stroked his mustache slowly. "Like Lamont," he said.

"The law," Matt said, "lays the same weight on everybody. You and Lamont, Ezra Meecham and Abe."

"Cole Pitman and Dave Morgan?"

74

"Everybody," Matt repeated. "You too, Hewitt." He turned and walked through the bar to the front door. It was a single affair, not like Lamont's fine double batwings, and it opened outward to give more room to the bar inside. When Matt pushed it, someone grunted on the other side. He stepped through.

"Sorry — oh, Jake."

"Listen," Jake Dill bawled, "Lippy told me, and I ain't coming into this town Saturdays without my gun. You fixin to have me shot?"

Matt sucked at his cigarette. "Not unless I do the shooting," he said quietly. "Everyone else will check his gun."

"I ain't going to do it!" Dill stood belligerently, hands on hips, in front of Matt. "I come to tell you that." His eyes were small and dark and angry. "You may be sheriff to Parkis, but you ain't to me."

Matt started past him, swung suddenly, and pinned him against the wall of the building. With one hand he slapped Jake Dill's arm aside and with the other reached for the man's gun. Dill swung a lopping blow that Matt turned on his shoulder. Matt brought up his forearm, catching Dill under the chin and making his head bounce against the wall. He got the gun and pulled it free. Stepping back, he let Dill loose.

"I'll check this at my office," he said quietly. "It'll be there when you're ready to leave." He stared into Jake Dill's flushed face; neither man moved. Then Dill's eyes dropped, and he jerked open the door to Hewitt's.

Matt said, "Make it tough and there'll be no guns any time, Jake," and he went across the street.

He paused before Bill Lamont's, watching a light breeze swirl dust in the streets. It was unusually warm and dry for so late in the fall, and until overdue rains came the dust would be like this. Crossing the street he had taken a fine powdery coating over his trouser legs, and he paused to brush it away.

Pushing open the doors of the saloon, he went into the big cool room. The building was a full two stories, and upstairs Lamont had his office and living quarters, with an additional suite that was reserved for Cole Pitman. Matt knew Lamont's habits well enough to be sure that he would be in his office at this time of day, winding up his breakfast with one of the fancy cigars he ordered by the gross and reading the old city newspapers he had freighted in.

Mounting the narrow stairs, Matt went

along an equally narrow hallway to a door at its end. "Come," Lamont called, in answer to his knock.

Matt pushed open the door and stepped into the office. It was a big room with fancy Indian rugs on the floor, varnished and rubbed walls with a number of hunting trophies on them, and not much furniture. There was a fireplace, cold now, with two chairs drawn up near it; a desk that looked onto the alley through the rear window; and, in shadow across the room, a settee where Lamont could take an evening nap.

Lamont was a big man and handsome, with his interlaced black and white goatee and mustache setting well on his dark strong face. He had even teeth that he liked to display in a swift smile, whether the smile had any meaning or not. His eyes were a deep brown, small and given to boring into a man. They bored into Matt now.

"Sit down, Sheriff." Lamont flashed his smile. "I wondered when you'd get around to me." He had been reading newspapers and now he folded them neatly with his strong well-kept hands and set them to one side of the desk. Picking up a lighted cigar from an ornate tray, he leaned back in his chair.

Matt took the leather-bottomed chair

beside the desk. After hooking one long leg over the other, he rested his broad-brimmed hat on his knee. He shook his head as Lamont pushed a cigar humidor toward him.

"Drink?"

"No. Thanks."

"Can't bribe you, eh?"

Matt smiled with his mouth, leaving his eyes cool. "No."

Lamont moved his neat hands in irritation. "Have I broken any laws yet?"

"There aren't many laws yet. Only keeping the peace."

"You can stretch that a long way," Lamont observed.

Matt nodded. "I intend to. I'm stretching my territory a long way, too. In time, I aim to see that the peace is kept on the benches and as far up as Shackville."

"Which side of Shackville, this or the other?"

Matt had to grin a little. "The other. If we ever get a county, Shackville will be part of it."

"You worry about Shackville, then, and tell me what this keeping of the peace adds up to."

Lamont puffed on his cigar, waiting for Matt to give his answer. When Matt said, "No liquor to drunks; no guns on Saturday

78

nights," he smiled and shook his head.

"How do I prove a man is drunk, Matt?"

"A drunk man is usually a mean man. If Bee Clancy had a drunk in her place she'd get rid of him for her own protection. It's for your protection to ease them away from your bar."

Lamont smiled again. "What if I made a mistake and serve a drunk?"

"You'll be warned," Matt said. "We haven't enough strangers in this country for you to be fooled often. You'll get a warning. One."

"One," Lamont murmured. "And the second time?"

"I'll close you up," Matt said flatly. He had not thought of the penalty before, only of the law itself. But logically it seemed to him that the penalty should be such that the concept of the crime was understood by those who committed it.

"You'd take a man's livelihood?"

"Temporarily," Matt said. He rose, nodding down at Lamont. "Long enough for him to see the error of his ways."

"You have the star," Lamont said. "And you have the title, Sheriff." His eyes smiled now. "But you haven't got the strength. There isn't a sharp edge to your lawmaking."

"Sharp edge or not," Matt answered, "my law can cut quick and deep." He put on his hat and walked with his deliberate stride to the door and out.

By dark, Matt had seen all of the townsmen but Ezra Meecham, who followed banker's hours, and he had found almost everyone in approval of his law against guns in town on the night that men tended to become the meanest. There was definite opposition to refusing liquor to a drunken man, but Matt left them complaining, understanding that it took time for most persons to become adjusted to something new.

Abe called him, as he went past the store, and he turned in. Abe said, "Matt, I found some of the men willing to help pay for a deputy for you."

"I planned on letting things run themselves until afternoons," Matt told him, "and then take over until the saloons close."

"And let every heller come to town mornings just to show you up?" Abe pointed out. "You see about a deputy."

"I'll do that," Matt said. He spoke cautiously. He would have to find a man he could trust; otherwise a deputy could play politics and set him back more than if he had none at all. "I'll think it over, Abe."

"He'll be paid fifty dollars and found," Abe added.

Matt nodded good night and walked next door to Daisy's place. The few middle-of-the-week customers had finished eating and were already at Lamont's or Hewitt's, leaving the room empty except for Daisy herself. She was wiping down the counter when Matt seated himself.

"One plate of hash is all that's left," she said. She was a buxom woman, big-framed, with hair the color of brass because it had been dyed so often. Her dark skin and eyes belied her present claim to blondness. She was a fine cook, even if she did sometimes remember her Spanish mother's teaching and overspice things.

"What did you have earlier?" Matt asked.

"Hash," Daisy said.

"I'll take hash," Matt said gravely.

Daisy brought a plate of it with thickening gravy on top. She slid bread and butter down the counter to him and followed them with coffee in a thick mug.

Daisy was able to smile even when weariness made her limp, but now she was sober-faced as she said, "I like your laws, Matt. Don't let them talk you down."

"Who?" Matt asked. He took a bite of hash and blew a gusty breath. "Water!"

Daisy laughed and gave him water. She rested her elbows on the counter. "Some of the townsmen," she said. "They're making a lot of fun over the laws."

"The jail's open, and everyone is invited," Matt said. He swallowed more water, wiped his eyes, and attacked the hash again. "Met the new people yet?"

He was not asking out of a desire for idle conversation but because he knew and respected Daisy's judgment. Her quick dark eyes had a way of seeing things in people that it took Matt longer to find.

"Saw you with the woman last week," she said. "She was in here for lunch one day. She's pretty and a lady, that's easy to see." She smiled, showing a gold tooth. "What will Lucy Morgan say?"

"Lucy Morgan was taken up with Cole Pitman at the last dance," Matt said. "People have stood around since and buried my chances. Why dig them up now?"

Daisy clucked her tongue. "And she went with Cole after he took Double M land."

"It's up to Lucy to judge the right and wrong of it," Matt said. To take the edge off his rebuke, he added, "Seen Adam Bede yet?"

"Ah," Daisy agreed mockingly, "ain't he the fancy one! He was in wanting rare roast beef — 'A center slice, my good woman.' He got hash."

Matt blew on his coffee. "Did you tell him he won't get beef until the next time your beau butchers a Morgan cow, Daisy?"

She half turned her head toward the kitchen but stopped the motion short. "Don't let Jud hear you say that, Matt. Jud is mighty sensitive. And nothing has ever been proved."

Matt laughed at her. "They found beef quarters hanging back of his cabin. Jud should be jailed." He nodded toward the door in the rear wall. "Tell him to come on in, Daisy. It happened before I took over as sheriff. It's not up to me to arrest him — yet."

Daisy looked thoughtfully a moment at Matt and then called, "Jud, you come in here!"

There was a thumping sound, and finally a man filled the doorway and came through into the room. He nodded gingerly at Matt, took a stool at the end of the counter, and looked plaintive until Daisy brought him a cup of coffee.

"Don't pick on Morgan cows all the time," Matt said, with heavy amusement. "Give Cole Pitman a break once in a while."

Jud Keppel grinned. He was a mountain

of a man, big in the middle but narrow top and bottom, so that he looked somewhat like a potbellied stove. His head was small for his body, his doughlike features seemed vacant, especially when he smiled, and his expression was as deceptive as his soft odd words. Matt knew that behind the washed-out eyes there was a sharp brain, but one that could see no good in settling down like other men to pile up money just for the sake of doing it.

He was a rebel who had drifted into the country and had gone to work for Morgan during Matt's first summer there. A handy man with horses and stock, he had taught Matt a good deal during the roundup. Later he had worked for Tim Ross, and once he had found a small pocket of rich ore back in the mountains. But he had never worked for one man, not even himself, for long at a stretch, preferring to take his wages and stretch them over idleness as long as they lasted.

Jud swallowed hot coffee and grinned again. "It wasn't much of a cow, Matt. Just an itty-bitty one that got lost. There it was, bawling and scared, and I just put it out of its misery."

"You seem to find a lot of lost stock, Jud."

Jud spread thick hamlike hands in a shrug.

"A man has to eat." He had a voice that was high-pitched but without sharpness. "If ranchers get careless with their cows, I ain't one to complain."

"From now on," Matt said, "I'll have to run you in if I catch you."

"That's fair warning," Daisy said. "You be more careful, Jud."

The big man giggled and buried his face in his cup. Matt rose, sighing. He knew that it was a game with Jud Keppel. Jud would have more than Morgan and Pitman men to dodge, now; he would have the law as well. And it would give him pleasure to sit in the hills and think of ways to get around them all.

Matt thanked Daisy for the meal, nodded to them both, and strolled out. The night was not sharp, even this late in the season; that worried Matt. When the cold came, it would come all at once, biting, dangerous, followed and led by heavy snows. He paused to roll a cigarette, turning his thoughts to the present, away from the future. The middle of the week was a fairly quiet time, and he was glad of the chance to accustom the town to his new ideas before Saturday. He looked up and down, decided on the route that would take him past each place in town an even number of times, and started out.

There was darkness all along the upper east side of Main, except for Daisy's, and her light went out while he stood debating. Across the street a lantern, turned low, hung outside the livery barn, and a lamp shone through the window of Sam Garton's freight office, but the hardware store and the bank were as dark as Abe Parkis'.

Matt crossed the street, saw that Garton was at work over his ledgers, and passed on. The night man at Colban's was asleep with his feet propped on the cold heater. Matt walked on steadily, past Ira Morris' hardware and the bank, through the dust of Hill, and on to Lamont's. Night moisture had come up through the ground, dampening the dust slightly in spots so that dark streaks were visible in front of the saloon where the yellow splashes of light struck the street.

Matt did not go in to Lamont's. There was only the noise of the piano and shuffling feet and under it, like a soft current, the sounds of gambling and men's muted voices. He recrossed Main, looking into the lobby of the hotel. Lippy had deserted it, leaving an old cowbell for summoning him if someone should come in and want a room. Matt knew that Lippy's sleep was safe. Outside of a cowboy too tired or too drunk to ride home, no one would come to the hotel at this hour.

At Hewitt's Matt opened the door and stepped inside. There were three men standing quietly at the bar. They all turned, as did Hewitt, who stood facing them.

"Evening, Sheriff," Hewitt said dryly. He lifted a tattered book and placed it on the counter. Thumbing it open, he ran his finger down a page with great pretense of concentration. "Joe Baltis, here, had two whiskeys. These other two have stuck to beer, and since I figure a dozen per man is safe they got six to go yet." He closed the book and looked unblinkingly at Matt.

"Just don't feed one man another man's share," Matt said, with equal dryness. He turned and left. His sense of humor was strong enough for him to appreciate the joke, but only for a moment. Irritation set in and stayed until he was on his final round and coming back toward Lamont's.

Hewitt's lights had gone out, and the only other activity was across the street where two men came from the big saloon. One of the men led the other shakily out to where their horses were tied at the hitch rail. The first man helped his partner into the saddle, settled himself on his own horse with an effort, all the while glancing at Matt standing nearby, and finally led the way south, out of town. Matt could not help laughing when the men, once past the laundry that marked the town limits, let out defiant whoops that rang on the cooling night air.

Lamont's lights went out soon afterward, and Matt turned homeward. He found himself thinking of Gail Winter and her reason for coming here. Despite her statement that she was a schoolteacher, she had not explained herself satisfactorily, and he still wondered to what part of Gaptown she belonged. It would not have bothered Matt — he was accustomed to taking people at their face value — except for what Abe had said about her. But it was not a thing he could ask bluntly, and he forced thoughts of her away.

CHAPTER SIX

On Friday, with only Lamont's saloon awake, Matt met trouble. The town was quiet, but with the quietness that comes before violent lightning. Matt, on edge, was making his second trip through the alley that ran past the rear of the jail. Daisy's tiny residence behind her restaurant was dark, and so was the rear of Abe's store down at the corner. Matt had the habit by now of glancing automatically into darkened rooms, and so he caught the movement he would have missed had he hesitated.

It was slight, a displacement of shadow more than anything else. It might well have been one of the cats that Abe kept for mousing, but Matt was too conscientious to go on without checking, and he stepped closer.

There was a small glass window in the rear door, and he peered through it to the inside. The movement was not repeated, and he stood still. Knowing what he would do all the time, he waited a full minute and then, taking out his key ring, clicked back the heavy lock.

With the noise of the lock he heard a rustling. Giving the door a quick jerk, he plunged inside, brought himself up short, and swung into deep shadow. He throttled his own breathing, holding himself erect by pressing his back against the rough board wall. His hand was by his gun but he held back his draw, waiting.

The shadows moved and then resumed their shapes. Matt closed his eyes and opened them again, and this time the shadows were motionless. The rustling noise was repeated; Matt located it in the front part of the storeroom, cut off from the rear room by a curtained doorway.

Gun in hand, Matt walked openly over the unplaned planks of the floor and reached for the curtain. Crumpling the edge in one hand, he jerked it back hard. The curtain ripped loose from its rod and fell to the floor. Tossing it aside, Matt stood in the open, still waiting.

There was an incautious breath that broke into a sob, and Matt spoke.

"Come out or get shot."

"I'll come." It was a high voice, trembling and without nerve. Even so, Matt kept his gun handy until footsteps brought a shadowy form level with him and then past him. He pressed the gun muzzle against a small back.

"Raise your hands," he ordered, without gruffness.

Short arms raised, and Matt reached out, taking a gun from a hip holster. With a few quick pats, he satisfied himself that his captive had no other weapon. "Now," he said, "walk into the alley."

After locking the door, Matt went on down to the city office, pushing his prisoner ahead of him. There, Matt lighted a lamp. "Sit down," he said gently. "Sit down, Toby."

It was a boy. He was small and dark with the peaked look that came from a diet of beans and salt pork and too much liquor for his age. Matt knew that he was twenty-one or thereabouts, though he was sure the boy had no better idea than he. His father, Jake Dill, never mentioned Toby's mother, and it was doubtful if Toby knew anything of her himself.

He said reluctantly, "I should have rid on." His eyes were sullen. "Let me ride, Matt. I was leaving this country anyway."

"Where to?" Matt asked pleasantly. He sat behind his desk, placed both guns in full view on its top, and passed the boy his tobacco. Matt was more concerned for the boy than afraid of him, and so he pushed the guns to one side where they were as handy to Toby as to himself.

"Any place. Maybe into Oregon or down to Nevada. I got a good horse."

"Getting a stake at Abe's?"

Toby licked first his lips and then the cigarette he had rolled. He returned Matt's tobacco. "Thought I would. Jake come home liquored and tried to beat me up. I told him his danged mine wouldn't pay, but because I didn't dig over fifty cents' worth he tried to whang me. I'm sick of it."

"He didn't hit you." There were no signs of fight on the boy.

"Not this time. I put a pick handle to his skull and rode out," Toby explained. "He'll come after me when he wakes up."

"Have supper?"

"I ain't had breakfast or dinner today — nothing but coffee. When Jake gets liquored, he forgets the grub."

Matt stood up. "Let's go to my place and eat."

Toby said suspiciously, "You going to lock me up or turn me loose?"

"I was thinking of feeding you first."

Toby remained seated, his thin mouth hard and tight in his dark face. "I ain't going to tell on Jake none," he said. "We ain't never got along, but that don't mean I'm going to tell anything."

Matt made no pretense of ignorance. Jake Dill was too closely associated with Shackville and with occasional robberies and murders. Matt knew that Toby was not beyond such things, but he had always regarded the boy with pity. Toby had too quick a mind for Matt to wish to see him follow Jake Dill.

"What Jake did isn't my business," Matt said. "What he does from now on is what concerns me. Let's go."

Toby stood up, retaining his suspicion while Matt holstered his own gun and thrust the other beside it in his belt. He followed Matt in silence to the three-room house and stood in the kitchen while Matt made a pot of coffee, cut thick slices of bread and cold beef, and put these things on the table with canned milk. They sat down.

Toby ate steadily and silently, wolfing nearly a loaf of bread and a good share of the beef before he raised his head. Matt loafed along on one sandwich and coffee, watching Toby eat and turning things over in his mind.

He could let Toby ride out, and he might be doing the boy a favor. Or he might be giving him free rein to carry what he had learned from his father on to Nevada or Oregon — and for his knowledge, he would get a bullet from men quicker to anger than those around Gaptown. He could do this, or he could accept the chance to prove one of his own theories.

"I can give you a job, Toby," he said, when the boy eased up in his eating.

Toby's lips twisted sourly. "Cleaning jail?"

"I mean it," Matt said. "You're trail-wise and mountain-smart. You can handle a gun. Fifty dollars and found. Deputy. You can bunk with me and eat at Daisy's."

Toby was full of food, and the sullenness had erased itself from his eyes. Now he looked at Matt, half in amusement, half in surprise. "Matt, you're crazy. I'm Jake Dill's boy."

"I'm Tim Ross's boy. If he was alive and he broke the law, I'd jail him. If he didn't break the law, I'd let him alone. You can treat Jake the same. Don't ride him and don't favor him."

"They'll laugh you out of town, Matt." Toby lifted his coffee cup and drank. "My star wouldn't carry no weight."

Matt said impatiently, "With me behind it, it'll carry as much weight as mine." He laid Toby's gun on the table. "Better roll in. Take the top bunk in the bedroom. I'll put your horse in the livery — if you're staying."

Toby rolled a cigarette and licked it slowly. He lifted his gun and pushed it into his holster. He said, "My horse is back of the hotel, Matt."

The next day, Matt sat his sorrel gelding at the foot of the hill beside the dark bulk of the abandoned laundry. It was Saturday, and he was expecting both Pitman and Morgan crews to come into town before it grew much darker.

The sun set early these fall days, dropping behind a pale sheet of sky over the cloudless mountains. The dust would hang in the air so that a rider's path was visible for a long distance unless the dark shut it out. It was nearly dark now, and Matt barely made out the first men, hearing the hoofbeats before he saw the figures top the hill and start down the slope.

It was a group of seven, and Matt made out Dave Morgan in the lead only when they had come within speaking distance. Morgan sat straight in his saddle, riding easily, like a man with no cares.

Matt moved his horse, blocking the trail just where it became Main Street. "Rein up, Dave," he ordered softly. "All guns have to be checked."

Dave Morgan pulled his deep-chested black to a halt, holding up his hand to stop the men single file behind him. Even in the dimness Matt could see the frosty smile on his face.

"I heard about your law, Matt, but a law isn't much good unless all men respect it."

"And you won't?"

"I will," Dave Morgan countered, "if others will. But I'll take no chances on getting my men shot up when they can't defend themselves."

"Pitman and his crew will check their guns," Matt said. "I'm here to see that they do."

A ripple of soft laughter broke from the men behind Morgan. Pat Ryan, Double M foreman, said, "Can't you see Pitman saying, 'Help yourself, Sheriff. Help yourself!' "

The laughter spread from a ripple into open guffaws. Only Dave Morgan did not laugh. He said simply, "The Morgans have always believed in some law, Matt. Maybe this is the right one. But we'll sit back and wait on this deal."

"Put your men over there," Matt said. He indicated a cleared space beside the wall of the laundry.

"We'll give up our guns when Bar Cross does," Morgan said. "All right, boys, we'll wait and think about the pleasures awaiting us." He drew out the last words so that the men rode to the cleared space laughing instead of grumbling.

Matt nodded to Dave Morgan. "Thanks. Now move back. I want to handle this alone."

There wasn't much of a wait. The Double M horses scarcely had time to grow restless when Cole Pitman led his men over the top of the hill. Saturday night was so ritualistic to the ranchers and miners of the country that Matt could almost judge to the minute when each group would appear.

"Cole," Matt said, when they had arrived,

"you'll check your guns."

Cole Pitman drew rein. "Evening, Sheriff." His voice was resonant with good humor.

"You can ride with me to the office," Matt said. He sat his sorrel crosswise of the trail, effectively blocking it except from a direct charge, and putting him crooked in the saddle when he faced the Bar Cross.

"You aren't mistaking me for a fool, Matt?"

"Morgan is waiting to do the same," Matt answered. "You have no choice."

Texas Zinker rode forward, crowding alongside Pitman. "Let Morgan keep his guns; we'll do the same. I said before, if a man wants to fight he's going to do it."

"I'll take your guns or you ride home thirsty tonight," Matt said, in the same level voice.

The sound of muttering spread back along the line of Bar Cross riders, swelling like a wave of wind riding the crowns of the forest.

"What's to stop us from riding as we are?" Cole Pitman asked. The amusement was gone from his deep voice, and Matt sensed the challenge lying bare in it. "Not you?"

"Maybe us," Dave Morgan said from the shadows.

"No," Matt said quickly. "Keep back. This

97

is my affair. It's my law, and I'll enforce it."
He shifted closer to Cole Pitman, his voice flat and emotionless.

"I'm the law, and if you ride me down there'll be more law. No man can fight that forever, Cole. Give me your guns."

There was a stillness, all men waiting. Out of the south a faint breeze stirred the dust of the trail, throwing pale spurts into the night air. The only other sounds were those of the horses — their restless shuffling, the creaking of saddle leather, the jangling of mouth bits.

Cole Pitman was the first to speak. "For tonight you win, Sheriff. Next time we'll know what to do."

Matt leaned away, hiding his sigh. "Next time," he said, in a pleasant tone, "will be taken care of when it comes. Let's ride to my office."

He knew that he hadn't won anything. This graceful giving in on the part of both the Bar Cross and Double M was no more than a respite. Cole Pitman wanted no sheriff to interfere with the plans he had been building step by step, slowly, over the years since he had come. Morgan, perhaps not against the law, could see no choice but to stay armed as long as Pitman was near. Matt understood this, and so he rode warily as they started toward the saloons.

Cole Pitman said, "I want Morgan at my side." They rode in two files like partners in a fantastic dancing march, Double M men paired with Bar Cross riders along the line until the last, where the four extra Pitman men rode alone.

The people on the streets, miners and loggers and millmen walking south of Hill and the few strolling townspeople north of the dividing line, were treated to the sight of the two crews riding parallel with Matt Ross leading them. They talked and laughed across at each other, but there was no man who let his hand stray far from his gun. Even now, a word, a wrong gesture, could throw a spark, and none wanted to be asleep if it lighted the fuse.

Matt reined in at the city office and, without looking back, strode into his office. Toby was behind the railing that divided the room, his thin dark face yielding no smile.

"We'll check their guns," Matt said. "Where are those tags I made up?"

"In the drawer," Toby said. "There's been trouble, Matt."

"Later," Matt said impatiently. "I'm holding a short fuse right now." He raised his voice. "All right."

Cole Pitman was the first to give up his gun. He did it with his usual grace, smilingly watching as Matt wrote his name on a paper tag and wired it to the guard of the forty-four. He turned and went out, making no comment.

Dave Morgan followed, scratching his dark head perplexedly. "This isn't wise, Matt. You can't cork an opened bottle of champagne to save it."

"What do you know about champagne?" Matt demanded humorously. "Lamont doesn't serve it."

"I'll bring you some when the Bar Cross is dust," Dave Morgan said in a heavy voice. "Or sprinkle it on your grave."

Matt waved him aside as Texas Zinker came into the room. If the foreman had any feelings, he kept them hidden by his thick beard. Matt did not relax, even though this appeared easy, until the last man had checked his gun and gone from the room. All of the time Toby had stood quietly to one side; no one commented on his presence or on the star he wore on his vest.

"Our first round," Matt said.

"Not with Jake," Toby answered. "He was here. I heard him coming, and I met him with a gun to his belly."

"He's in town?"

"No," Toby said. "He rode out again." His thin face twisted with distaste. "He was half drunk when he came, Matt. There's no good in my father. He went out with threats, and he'll go to Shackville and come back to make those threats good. He remembers my using a pick handle on him, and it won't let him rest."

"I'll watch out for him," Matt promised.

Toby sat on the railing that divided the room. He rolled a cigarette with deliberate care, and when he had it licked and lighted he said, "I'd better ride like I wanted to, Matt."

"I don't want a coward for a deputy," Matt said. He shrugged and turned his back, bending to the task of hanging the guns on a rack he had built for the purpose.

"Coward!" Toby cried. "I ain't afraid. It's just that no man likes to think of a shoot-out with his father."

"Nor a father with his son," Matt said. He did not look up. He felt as old as Abe Parkis or even Ezra Meecham. But there was a strong stubbornness in him that refused to admit he had misjudged Toby.

"Jake ain't a real father," Toby said.

Matt finished his work and straightened. "You patrol, Toby. I'll see to Jake for now."

Toby turned his cigarette in his lips. "For

now, for now," he said softly, and walked from the room.

Matt left the lamp burning, turning it low, and went into the night. He took his horse across the street to Luther Colban's livery, leaving it with the stablehand. He crossed back, going to Daisy's.

She was serving late, as she always did on Saturdays, and there were three customers at the counter when Matt entered. He ate slowly, in order that he might still be there when the others had gone. They left before he reached his coffee and pie, and he called Daisy toward him.

"Jud coming in tonight?"

"He's in," Daisy said. "He's at Hewitt's with his miners." She smiled, showing her gold tooth. "Jud's all right, Matt." She reached under the counter and brought up four guns. "They're his and his men's."

"Jud's all right as long as you're around," Matt agreed.

"He'll do what I tell him," Daisy said.

Matt got up and reached across the counter to a box of cigars. He took one and settled back. "Just don't tell him the wrong thing," he suggested.

Daisy drew herself a cup of coffee and leaned against the counter. "Jud's working up a crew, Matt. He's digging out a pocket on a creek up above Morgan's, and they'll be ready to ship to the trail soon."

"Jud's a good worker — when he'll work."

Daisy sipped her coffee, speaking over the rim of the cup. "It's a good crew. Jud got 'em out of the shacks back of the livery. They been rotting there all summer."

"Jud did?"

"All right," Daisy said, "maybe I thought of it for him." She looked at Matt, her dark eyes serious. "I'm telling you because they like Jud. They'll do almost anything for him. He treats 'em decent. Like partners."

Matt lit his cigar and stood up. "Get to it, Daisy."

She looked a little embarrased, something Matt had not seen before. "Starting laws is hard," she said finally. "There's lots of people against you. If you need help any time ——"

Matt smiled his sincere pleasure. "Thanks, Daisy. And thank Jud. It just might come to that. I hope it doesn't, but it might."

He went out, going to the west side of Main Street and down. On Saturdays he was to take the west side of Main and Toby the east. They had planned it that way, and they hoped to make it work.

Crossing Hill Street, he thought of what Daisy had told him. It was a good feeling to know that someone was behind you. It took away a little of the lonesome feeling a man had when he walked the knife-sharp crease between two groups lined up against each other. And he was glad it was Jud Keppel, who would bother no one until he was asked.

Matt turned in at Lamont's. The saloon was filled with men; they were thick at the bar, and their noise and sweat and dust crowded the dance floor. Early though it was, the dancing girls were on duty. Matt watched them a moment, bare arms and short dresses catching the glint of the hanging oil lamps as they swirled in and out of time to the scraping of the three-piece orchestra. Matt walked around the dance floor, between it and the bar, and left them to their labors.

He eyed the men along the bar. For the most part they were Bar Cross men in front and Double M toward the rear. Between them, like a weak-walled fortress, were a few loggers and a scattering of miners. Matt saw no gun on anyone, and so he drifted past the end of the bar and turned toward the gambling tables.

Smoke hung low and thick beneath the ceiling, pressing down on the tables and half obscuring the silent intentness of the players. Over those green-topped tables, men bent with a concentration that they achieved at no other time. Waiters moved in and out, serving drinks. There was a scattering of girls beside the men, brought there for luck or, perhaps, to hoodoo an opponent.

Still Matt saw no guns on display. He reached a far corner and came onto Cole Pitman and Adam Bede, who was costumed as flamboyantly as he had been on his arrival. They were at a small table, an uncut deck between them. They were drinking beer and talking, seeming to have no use for the cards in front of them.

Matt nodded pleasantly, went by, and turned back. "Sometimes a man has a gun under his coat," he said, making it sound like a question.

Adam Bede smiled, showing his strong teeth. "A custom, I am told, developed by those dealers who also carry an extra ace up their sleeve. Have no fear, Sheriff, I'm completely bereft of firearms."

"All that long talk means you have no gun," Matt observed.

Cole Pitman raised a laughing face. "I admire words like that, Sheriff."

Matt studied him narrowly. "He has more than words. I've seen him unseat Jake Dill

105

from his horse and not wrinkle a coat sleeve."

"It's a good thing to know about a man," Pitman conceded. "Especially of a friend."

Matt nodded and passed on. He had, he realized, taken a liking to the flamboyant Bede, and it was no pleasure to find him talking to Pitman. Nor in having Pitman call him friend. But it would have to wait, Matt thought. It was too early to judge Bede, just as it was too early to judge Gail Winter. Matt hunted for Lamont, finding him by the roulette wheel. Lamont gave him a quick glance and then jerked his head.

Matt followed him up to the office where the noises from below were drowned by distance. Lamont poured a drink and, when Matt refused, tossed it off himself. He leaned back in his chair.

"Everything is smooth here. You'll find me cooperating."

"How far? How long?"

"I have a safe full of guns now," Lamont said.

"What happens when a man gets liquored and wants more?"

"Then I'll steer him from the source of supply into the sobering influence of the night air." Lamont smiled. "What more can you ask?"

"Nothing more," Matt admitted. "I see the new man downstairs. Have you hired him yet?"

"I'm thinking about it," Lamont said. "But he's too windy for me."

"A man doesn't deal with his mouth," Matt said dryly.

"A friend of yours?"

"Any man is better working than being idle," Matt said.

Lamont ducked his head in a nod and chuckled. "I'll hire all indigents, Sheriff."

Matt could not like this man, despite the charm and frankness he showed — perhaps because of it. Matt said, "You're windy, too."

"A new man and a new woman," Lamont observed, almost idly. "Is she employed, too?"

"She came as a schoolteacher. We need one." Matt waited, knowing what might come now and not wanting it. Particularly not wanting it to come from Lamont's mouth.

"Then," Lamont said easily, "she had better stay away from Bee Clancy's."

"That's not our concern."

"It might be — to parents."

"It's no way to judge a woman."

"It's the kind of thing that makes for a quick judgment," Lamont pointed out. "It

107

seems that you're as fond of her as you are of Bede, Matt."

Matt stood up. "Make quick judgments, and you'll wish for your words back," he said.

Lamont's laugh was his answer, and he could only turn away and walk out. Lamont's voice followed him.

"I hope your law-making is sharper than your experience, Matt." His laughter kept pace with Matt as he went on down the stairs.

CHAPTER SEVEN

Matt went through Lamont's to the alley and worked his way up it toward Hill Street. The few shacks that Bill Lamont owned spilled light into the alley nearly the full distance to Bee Clancy's. Out of them came noise, laughter, and an occasional curse. But up close to Hill there was a heavy silence.

Bee Clancy's faced forward to Hill Street. Ezra Meecham had built it well, chinking the pine logs solidly and sealing it over inside. Thus the sounds that came from it were always muffled, and, since the windows were always well shuttered and covered with heavy draperies, there was as little light as noise.

Matt kept himself alert despite the light coming from behind him. He knew the possibilities of ambush, especially on Saturday night, and so he walked softly and carefully, his eyes moving constantly, his footfalls muffled by the softness of the dust.

Because he was quiet and watchful, he heard the couple before they heard him. They were in shadow, blending into it against the side of Bee Clancy's. He heard the low murmur of voices, faint ripples on the layers of night sounds, but not until he was close by did he realize that both voices were in a higher key than a man's.

He stopped where he was, trying to decide what next to do. One voice was rich and strong and, though too low in tone for him to make out the words, easily identified. Otherwise he would have gone forward and nodded and continued past to Hill. But because it was Gail Winter, he hesitated. He could not explain why even to himself, and the lack of understanding irritated him. He could, he knew, turn and retrace his steps, but that was distasteful to him. He did not condone evasion in anyone else and could not in himself.

After a moment of lingering, he stepped

forward. As he walked abreast of the shadows, a voice came quickly, startled, as if the owner had been too engrossed to pay attention to outside intrusions.

"Who is that?"

"Sheriff," Matt said, matter-of-factly. "Be careful here. It's a dark place."

"I can take care of myself," Gail Winter said irritably.

"As you wish," Matt replied. He walked on, leaving Gail Winter and her companion, whose voice he had not recognized. Turning the corner onto Hill, he passed the front of Bee's place and kept on slowly instead of doubling back and going up the alley to the rear of Sam Garton's freight station. He stopped beside the west edge of the vacant lot that extended to Main. He rolled a cigarette, and when he lighted the match it illumined the lines of worry in his face.

He dropped the match and put his boot toe on it. Decided now, he waited for Gail Winter to come along. Since he had left her, he knew he would wait. He did not hunt for his true reason, but spent the time searching for a reason acceptable to her.

It was only a short while before he heard her footsteps, strong and deliberate, on the boardwalk, concealing nothing nor brooking a man to block her path. He held his

110

ground, turning so that he faced her. When she neared, he drew deeply on his cigarette in order that she might identify him in the faint light. She was very tall against the darkness; a graceful woman, he thought.

She did not slow her pace. "I don't need your protection," she said.

When she was abreast of him, Matt turned, took her hand, put it on his arm, and walked with her. She made no effort to pull away, and they walked silently across Main, down to State, and turned north.

"I suppose you know that I've moved," she said.

"Everyone knows everyone else's business here," he answered. "You're at the parsonage now, I heard."

"As most of my pay for teaching — when it starts."

They crossed State and stepped to the tiny porch. Here she pulled away from him. She unlocked the door and went in, leaving the door ajar. He did not move except to drop his cigarette and step on it. When a lamp was lighted inside, Matt used the glow to find his cigarette butt and kick it from the porch. She returned to the doorway.

"Come in. You can't do your talking out there."

He stepped in, shutting the door. Holding

his hat in his hands, he was silent while she removed her coat and dropped it across a chair. The furnishings, he noted, were old but fairly comfortable. He recognized a number of pieces from other places and knew that they were all she had been able to get — things bought and sold by Ezra Meecham.

Having finished placing her coat, she faced him, her gray eyes inquiring. "You can stay awhile?"

"Awhile," he admitted.

"Then I'll make you some coffee," she said. She retreated to the kitchen. Matt placed his hat on a bare table beside the door and followed her. He saw that she was competent in building a fire for the coffee. When she had the water on to boil, he returned to stand in the parlor.

She came back, seated herself on the sofa, and nodded permission for him to follow suit. He did so, at the opposite end of the sofa, but turned so that he faced her.

"Now tell me I'm a fool," she said challengingly.

"That's not my place," he answered. "But there is talk about you having been seen at Bee Clancy's."

"Talk?" She shook her head. "I've never been inside. And whose business is it?" She sat quite calmly, her hands folded in her lap, but her eyes and her expression were as challenging as her voice.

Matt did not like it; it was not a thing to talk about to a woman, especially one that he scarcely knew. But she had begun it, so he said, "Everyone's business — in Gaptown. I heard it from Bill Lamont. He'll spread it around quickly enough."

"Is the word of a — a saloon man worth so much?"

He stirred. "That's not the point," he said half sharply. "Lamont or a stablehand or Abe Parkis' wife. It's gossip. It's their way of judging you. What things you do first. How else can they judge?"

"By my appearance. Do I look like someone from Bee Clancy's?"

He moved his hand impatiently. "No, or I wouldn't be here, bothering about it. You're a handsome woman, you know that. You show that you know it with every movement. And it's one of the things that will make other women listen more closely to Lamont's talk. You know that, too."

"I'm no child," she retorted. "Nor are you as simple as I thought." Her gray eyes were angry now, her full mouth a set line. "What I did tonight, and night before last — those things are my business."

"That won't help you keep a schoolteaching job," he said.

"I have my own money. The work isn't needed."

"Still, a schoolteacher is a fine thing. The people are pleased."

"Were pleased," she corrected him. There was sudden amusement on her face. "You weren't so pleased to find me in the alley."

"It wasn't my affair," he said. "But Saturday is a bad night. Men get drunk, and a few might have spoken to you. Thinking ____"

He stopped, and she laughed softly at his confusion. "I'm no child," she repeated. "I know what men think." She rose and picked up her coat. She took a derringer from the pocket and held it up for him to see. "I broke your law."

"I can overlook that." He smiled with relief at having had the subject changed.

"It isn't loaded," she said. Her laugh rippled through the room. "I have no bullets."

"I can get you some," Matt answered.

"I don't want them — yet."

He didn't like the way she had spoken, but before he could say anything she went into the kitchen, leaving him alone to think about it. When she returned with a small tray holding the coffee and cups, he had achieved nothing.

She set the tray on the table where his hat rested. "Cream?" She lifted his hat and dropped it on top of her coat.

"No," he answered. He motioned toward the chair where her coat and his hat were together. "I've been accused of being too friendly with you already."

She handed him his coffee. "By Lamont, too?"

"Yes." He let her carry the conversation, knowing that she would move in any direction she wished anyway. She was a strong-willed woman. He could feel it in her words, in her voice. His warning had no more than irritated her and, having disposed of the subject, she had pushed it aside before he was ready.

"Lamont is a friend of Cole Pitman?" She seated herself and sipped at her coffee. "Smoke if you wish."

Thanking her with a nod, he rolled a cigarette. "He's close to Cole. Do you know him?"

"I was just asking," she said quickly. "He's talked about a lot. He's a big man here, isn't he?"

Adam Bede had become friendly with Cole Pitman, and now Gail Winter asked about him. And in far too casual a way to satisfy Matt. He said, "Cole came here five years ago. He was a very young captain in the Union Army, so the story goes. They say he was mixed up in something in the South and left with a full carpetbag."

"It's plausible."

Matt studied her, but she was busy with her coffee. "Then," he said, "the carpetbag must have been very full — and of gold, not greenbacks. He came here with a lot of money. And he brought a sergeant of his company, Texas Zinker. They liked Morgan's east bench, so they took it. Zinker sent for a number of men, and they kept it from Morgan. There was no fighting, just Pitman's show of power. It was free land, actually. Morgan had no title." Matt smiled faintly. "In fact, he had withdrawn everything from it but a few scrubs. But it gave Pitman the idea he could push Morgan around. He's just getting into full swing now."

"This *Texas* Zinker was in the *Union* Army?"

"Some men," Matt said dryly, "will fight for what pays best."

"You don't like Cole Pitman or his men." She made it a statement of fact.

"That has nothing to do with my job

116

here," he said. "It's my belief that he killed my father — or had him killed. But our dislike is mutual."

"Your belief," she murmured. "And you've done nothing about it?"

"I have no proof," he said simply. "My father was freighting across Cole's land. Cole had given a warning, but he was a stubborn man."

"You have no proof," she repeated after him, in the same thoughtful, murmuring voice.

Matt felt scorn from her look. "Why are you goading me? Am I supposed to kill Pitman and look for proof afterwards?"

"You're the sheriff," she said.

"Then I, least of all, can break the law. That isn't equal justice."

"An eye for an eye is equal justice."

He could not understand why she made so much of the subject. Her gray eyes watching him so steadily made him uncomfortable. He drank his coffee and rose.

"If it's possible to keep away from Bee's, do so," he said to her. "Otherwise you might have people questioning your right to teach."

She rose too, handing him his hat. "I thought people here didn't ask questions."

"Mostly they don't," he said. "But they

117

think the answers to the questions they'd ask if they were the kind to ask them."

She smiled. "That's my warning again?" Opening the door, she said, "Thank you for walking with me."

"And thank you for the coffee." He would have said more, but the sound of gunfire rattled in the air, and a sickening sense of having failed this Saturday night, too, drove the words from his mind.

"Good night," he said quickly, and ran from the house. His footfalls were sharp and clear as he hurried down the boardwalk, and then they were gone as the dust engulfed them.

She did not close the door, but stood listening.

Matt ran across the street and alongside Mrs. Cowley's boardinghouse to the alley. Between Daisy's and the abandoned building separating it from the city office was a narrow space, and Matt ran that way. He came onto Main to face a whirl of dust as a rider put his horse through a circus act. He was firing a gun into the air and, at the same time, making his horse rear and paw the air with his forefeet.

"Jake!" Matt called out sharply. "Jake Dill!"

The horse and rider calmed down, and

Jake Dill stared at Matt with a triumphant grin on his face. The only other watchers were a few men who had run up from the saloons.

"Howdy, Sheriff. I came to tell you I was in town."

"Give me that gun."

Jake Dill laughed. "You're as bad as Toby — wanting things."

Matt heard running feet on the boardwalk behind him. Without turning, he said, "Get into the office." Toby went on by, and Matt continued to stare at Dill.

"Your gun, Jake. Now!"

"I'll keep my gun," Dill answered testily. His expression changed, and he roared with laughter. Matt realized that he was drunk.

"You go any farther down the street, and you'll spend the night in jail."

Dill swung his horse in toward Matt. "That's your law. It ain't mine." He wheeled away and started down Main.

Matt darted forward, moving more quickly than most of the watchers could remember having seen him move, and grasped the horse's bridle. Jake Dill turned a surly face downward and slashed at Matt's arm with the barrel of his gun.

"No," Matt said, and twisted aside.

"Damn you, Ross!"

119

The gun slashed again. Matt shot out his free hand and caught Dill's wrist. Stepping back, he released his grip on the bridle and pulled, letting all of his weight ride onto Jake Dill's wrist. The horse shied and moved skittishly away from Matt. His boot heels braced in the dust, Matt held his grip, letting the movements of the horse twist Dill's arm.

Howling, Jake Dill kicked his feet free of the stirrups and came over the horse's neck. Matt let loose as the man's bulk slid toward him, stepping back so that Dill rolled into the dust and came up sitting. Matt plucked the gun from his hand.

"Now," he said, "we'll go to jail."

Jake Dill put his hands in the dust behind himself and pushed. He got to his feet and stood, wavering, working to get his breath back into his lungs and, when he did, spitting dust from his mouth.

"I ain't going. Give me my gun, Ross. Damn you!" He was angry, with the near-tearful anger of too much liquor.

"You're drunk," Matt said coldly. "Get going."

"Put me there." Jake Dill thrust his face at Matt, anger sliding swiftly into belligerence. "You — Sheriff."

Matt tucked the gun into his belt. He

stepped forward, lifting one arm. Dill growled deep in his throat and put up his fists. Matt used his upraised arm to sweep Dill's hands aside and drove his other fist under them in a short sharp blow. Dill staggered backward, slipping to one knee as he tried to turn aside. Matt deliberately chopped his knuckles down on the back of Dill's neck, behind one ear, and then moved away, waiting.

Dill sat down, turning again as he fell so that he landed on his rump. He continued to sit, shaking his head and spitting drops of blood. Matt took his arm and lifted him. He clamped the arm up behind Dill's back in a hammer lock and moved the cursing man to the jail. The onlookers followed. Locking Dill in a cell, Matt returned to the steps of the city office.

"Go back to your drinking," he said shortly. "The show's over."

He went into the office. "Check this gun, Toby."

Toby came from the shadows by a window. He lowered a rifle from the sill of the window, which was open. "I never saw anyone handle Jake like that," he said. "You did it easy, Matt."

"Easy enough," Matt said, "when a man's that drunk."

"Them guys gawking got an eyeful," Toby said, pleased. "There won't be so many laughing at you from now on."

"Let's hope not," was all Matt said. He went out, making his rounds again. He met sullenness, not respect, in the saloons. It was one thing to have a law, another to see it in action. Matt recognized this kind of reasoning and put emphasis behind the way he looked over the men standing at the bars or thumping raggedly on the dance floor.

But for Jake Dill's visit, the town stayed comparatively quiet, and Matt knew they were saving it for another time, for a time when they might catch him off guard. At two A.M. he turned home for bed. The town was closed down except for a few still at Lamont's. They were the hangers-on, always the last to go, and their concern was with drinking all they were allowed, not in making trouble.

There was a feel of freezing in the air when Matt was aroused in the morning by hammering on his door. Day was coming in the windows, gray and ugly, and when he was fully awake he heard the steady drip of cold rain from the eaves of his house.

It was Ezra Meecham at the door. He came in with water dripping from his tat-

122

tered cold-weather buffalo coat. He blinked wetly at Matt, his face seamed with dissatisfaction. He was a withered man, and he looked ridiculous in the huge moth-eaten garment that enveloped him. His dissatisfaction showed in his eyes and in the way he carried his small body. He wore a broad-brimmed hat that was too big for his size, and he kept it on over his bald head.

"You got Jake Dill in jail," he said accusingly. His voice was high and screechy.

"He was drunk and disorderly," Matt said. He turned to the potbellied parlor stove and began to lay a fire. Ezra Meecham followed him, standing almost in the kindling box, his twisted fingers shaking wrathfully under Matt's nose.

"He ain't drunk and disorderly now. You got no right to keep him in."

Matt looked at the old clock on the wall. "You're excited for eight on a Sunday morning, Ezra," he observed. Touching a match to the paper and wood, he stepped back, closing the stove top as he did so. "And interested."

"You go putting a man in jail for a little drinking and hell raising, and there won't be no one in town. They'll go to Shackville. Then where'll business be? I've told 'em so. And this proves it."

Matt turned away in disgust from the raw voice. You couldn't argue with a man like Ezra. You couldn't push the clink of gold far enough away to make him hear anything else.

Matt said, "If a man like Jake Dill wants to take all his business to Shackville, that's fine. For me and for the town." He moved closer to the stove as it began to throw out warmth. "Jake isn't dying in there."

"You got no right to keep him any longer. Overnight is enough."

This was pressure, Matt thought. It was not much from just one man, but if Ezra Meecham got others behind him the pressure would grow until it pushed law to one side.

"Ezra," he said, "I'm the sheriff — right now. As long as I'm the sheriff I'll run the jail."

The old man jumped up and down in his anger, his voice shrill. "You're ruining business. You're ——"

Matt reached out and took a handful of heavy coat in his fist. "Ezra," he said mildly, "get out of here." With little effort, he propelled the old man out the door and onto the porch. "When I'm ready to let Jake out, he'll get out."

He shut the door and turned back to the

stove. He could hear Ezra Meecham screeching on the porch, but after a moment the noise ceased. Matt went into the kitchen and built a fire for his breakfast.

Saying he was the sheriff and being the sheriff, he found, could be two different things. Ezra and his gold were not much alone, but the fear of losing money drew men together as a magnet drew iron filings, and before long the old man might carry more power than his wizened size indicated.

CHAPTER EIGHT

Rain laid cold fingers on the land for two weeks before the skies broke. The clinging dust was washed from the air, leaving it clean and chilled. At night the gluelike mud of the trails was crusted over with a freezing, but in the daytime it thawed so that a man and horse sank fetlock-deep.

The snow waited until early December, and then it failed to stay. The whole countryside lay under white one day, and the next day the rain turned it back to brown sucking mud. But the freezes were harder and the thaws shorter each time, and the feel of winter was strong enough to make the laziest man saw and stack wood for his stoves.

Cole Pitman splashed his horse through the gummy trails and came into Gaptown, turning east at Hill and going past State around behind the church and the parsonage. It was a drab drizzly early evening. Few of the people outside paid any attention to the man hunched under his poncho, and none were about to see him dismount at the rear of Gail's house and wade to the door that opened onto the tiny backyard.

She answered his knock, peering uncertainly into the dusk.

Cole Pitman doffed his hat. "Can a man come in out of the wet?"

She waited a moment, silent, and then, shrugging, held the door for him. When he was inside, she shut it carefully and walked ahead into the parlor. The airtight stove was glowing, and Pitman dropped his hat and poncho, warming himself with his back to the heat.

He regarded her with an amused smile, saying nothing. He had done the calling; now it was up to her.

"I won't offer you coffee because I don't expect you to stay that long," she said, in an even voice. She wore a dull green dress that highlighted her thick golden hair. There was a neatness about her and about the room, broken only by a pile of school papers on a

126

small table. She kept her eyes on him while he took everything in.

"You lack hospitality," he said.

"For some, Cole," she admitted. "What is it you want?"

His smile sharpened swiftly. "To warm myself, Gail. It was a cold ride. I've been waiting for a chance to see you."

"You needn't have bothered." The antagonism was thick between them, and she let it stay that way, a barrier through which he could not push himself. She stood stiff and straight before him, not moving her gray eyes from his face.

"You're making it hard for me, Gail."

His polish never failed to amaze her; she thought of him as he could be, as he often was. She knew how easy it was to push him to the place where the polish was gone and the naked ugliness he hid was open for her to see.

"There's nothing you can do to me," she said, and waited.

"I've been here five years," he said softly. "I'm stronger than you." He curbed himself behind casualness. "I hear you're teaching the school."

"Yes."

"And seeing the sheriff." He laughed quietly. "Our very successful sheriff."

"He's good," she said simply. "If he'd been the law five years ago ——"

"I'll not listen to that!" He interrupted her harshly.

"But you will, Cole." She thought back and the anger came, rough and fast as it always did. It was like yeast, multiplying in time and darkness. "Your five years of growing strong don't yet reach up to your weakness."

"I have no weakness," he said impatiently. "I grow stronger every day."

"You always did make great boasts, Cole. You can't frighten me away with them."

His eyes were cold on her, though his mouth was smiling again. "A boaster is a man who fails. Remember that, Gail."

She moved brusquely. "Say what you have to, Cole. I have work to do."

"You told the sheriff why you came here?"

She could smile now. This was his reason for coming, and so his weakness still lay tender and exposed, not yet protected by the power he had built here. It gratified her to know this; she could feel no pity for this man, even though she knew he did as he did because inside he was driven. There was no other way for him.

"Why did I come?" she asked mockingly, softly.

"Damn you!" He raised his hand, but she did not move aside. He relaxed again, trembling a little with the effort of fighting for control of himself.

"You can go now," she said. Her eyes were bright on his face. "Go without any trouble."

He stepped forward, confronting her, his face inches from her own. The smoothness was completely gone now, back inside where she could not see it. The throbbing rawness of the past was plain for her to read. She did not give ground to him, but stood immobile. He was no taller than she, and so they were eye to eye.

"I'll have no interference from you."

She drew a quick harsh breath. And because she was a woman and knew her advantage, she pressed one hand to her breast in mock horror — and then she laughed. She threw back her head and let the sound ripple from her throat.

She could see that the laughter ran through him like a keen knife blade, and it was the reaction she had desired. She stopped laughing, but kept her smile. "Go home, Cole." Her voice held all of the contempt she could muster.

She knew his quick rages when he was like this. But she was not afraid. She wondered at this — perhaps it was the security of Matt's nearness. It was evening, and every evening he came here, sharing her supper and smoking his cigar before going quietly back to his business. This was the time she expected him, and Cole, knowing the gossip as he always did, would know that too.

He was quiet in anger until the force of it was too great for him to contain. He raised his arms and, when she did not flinch, brought them down on her shoulders.

"Maybe you need something to laugh at," he said harshly. He drew her to him, against him, with a quick movement of his powerful body. His hands slipped down to her upper arms and his fingers dug into her so that she went white under the sharp pain.

"Let me go!" she commanded, without hysteria.

"Something to laugh at," he repeated. He moved his head to reach her mouth, and when she twisted her face aside he pushed at her with his body, driving her toward the sofa, blind in his anger, hating her.

She spoke with the same imperious coldness, though now she was afraid. "Stop it, Cole. This is not Bee Clancy's. Nor am I Ellen."

He released her, stepping back. The fury was running across his face like dark clouds on a quick wind. "This has gone far enough. I'll not have you talking."

She rubbed her arms with palms damp with the sweat from her fear. While he talked, she walked around him. She moved as gracefully, as unruffled, as if he had not thrown his angry strength against her. At the chimney corner, she reached into the pocket of her coat hanging there and drew out her small derringer.

The metal was cold in her palm, but beyond that she had no feeling. That she would shoot to kill him, using bullets Matt had got for her, she accepted without question. She was no longer angry; she did not act in anger. The cold logic of her mind told her what might be necessary, and she accepted it.

She let him see the gun, the cold steel glittering in the light of the lamp. "Now you'll go," she said. "Neither of us will take orders from you."

His glance touched the gun and then her unsmiling face. He stood a moment, recovering himself, and then he bowed in his mocking manner and stepped to where he had flung his hat and poncho. He took time putting them on before he walked out.

She stood by the lamp, the gun waiting in her hand, and she did not relax until the sound of hoofbeats in the mud and rain faded beyond her hearing.

She sat on the sofa, weakness coming over her to replace the strength she had drawn on. She dropped the gun to the carpet, staring at it dully. When she was rested, she found that she could think, and her mind turned to Matt.

The clock said that it was close to seven, and he was more than an hour overdue. "I'm thinking like a wife," she told herself.

This could make her smile because she had had no word from Matt that would lead her to think that way. But her smile was gone with another thought.

Had Cole known that Matt would not come this evening?

And again, what would he do now that she had given him no satisfaction? She was here; she could expose his weakness whenever she chose. She had not backed down under his threats. And he was not the man to let one woman, one person, or one hundred persons stand in the way of his success. Some day his impatience would break through, and then the little gun would be of no more use than it had been before Matt brought her bullets for it.

Cole Pitman rode to the livery and left his

horse with the stableman. He walked to Bill Lamont's, ignoring the greetings of the few who passed him on the street. He was usually a civil man, but tonight he was as wrapped in his thoughts as the world was wrapped in rain, and he heard none of the greetings.

It was Saturday, but the damp weather had kept the town quiet up to now. Pitman shook rain from his hat and poncho as he pushed into Lamont's. The big room was nearly empty, and he had no trouble locating Texas Zinker at a side table.

Pitman ordered supper and ate it in silence, quickly and hurriedly, as if it were something to be done with before other matters were reached.

He took a cigar when the meal was cleared from the table. "I'm tired of holding Dill back," he said angrily.

"You're getting impatient again, Captain," Zinker said. "Your first plan is working out. The sheriff has no time to set himself, what with watching Dill or his men all the time and having to arrest one or the other of them now and then."

"It's still letting him stay in town," Pitman pointed out. "And it's getting so a lot of men are used to his laws." His scowl showed the impatience roweling him. "A man rides in and checks his gun with no more fight than a sheep. Even Lamont won't give a liquored man an extra drink."

"You can get Lamont to cut up a little," Zinker suggested.

"Maybe," Pitman answered. "But Bar Cross isn't everything to Lamont, even if it is his biggest customer. Nor are we everything to Ezra Meecham just because over half of his funds are from our deposits."

Texas Zinker looked oddly at his boss. "What are you getting at, Captain?"

Pitman said, "Even they could turn against us if the pressure got strong enough. We have to be bigger — we have to be worth more than the rest of the town and the range put together. We have to do it quickly."

"Ah," Zinker said, with slow realization. "You're thinking of power — and you're thinking of being respected."

Pitman spoke angrily. "Without respect your power is cut in half!"

"So it is," Zinker agreed. "You mean the girl who was at Bee Clancy's." He saw the admission form quickly on Pitman's face and then disappear. His laugh was short. "I know these things, Captain, even if you never saw fit to tell me."

"If you know, how many others do?"

Zinker shrugged. "You know better than

134

to think I talk. No others do — that I know of."

"There's one," Pitman said. He sounded relieved, as if it took away pressure to have someone to share his secret with. "That new schoolteacher."

Zinker nodded slowly, showing his understanding. "That's why you talked to her then — why you rode to see her." He laughed again briefly. "I watched you today, Captain. The sheriff has a habit of going to her place evenings. Is she that dangerous?"

"She was a child when I saw her last," Pitman said. "But a stubborn one, with the never-thinking stubbornness of the female. Now she's a woman, and she's equally as stubborn."

"And equally never-thinking," Zinker said dryly. "And also close to the sheriff."

"She hasn't told him anything," Pitman said. "I'm sure of that. And I don't want her to. I'm going to turn Dill loose, Texas. I want Ross kept busy, out of the way, out of town. I want time to take care of this woman — and I don't want his interference."

"All right," Zinker agreed. "The freight train will be coming down from the mines soon." His eyes glowed above his brown beard. "That will give Ross a reason to try and clean out Shackville. Let Bald Leggett keep him busy up there." He could see Pitman's quick mind catch the idea and shape it. "Dill tells Leggett what to do," Zinker went on.

"Maybe Dill can keep Ross busy looking for Morgan cows, too," Pitman said.

Zinker raised his hand, signaling for a drink. He said, "Just one thing, Captain. Ross has a deputy. What about Dill's boy? He's solid for Ross, and he knows Dill's ways."

Pitman's smile showed a little humor. "He's still Dill's boy, Texas." His smile became broader, letting Zinker see that he felt quite satisfied with himself. "As for your plan, Texas — I got that started with Dill some time ago."

Laughing, he picked up the drink Zinker had ordered for himself and downed it, lifting it first in a mock toast.

"To our sheriff, Texas."

That day, before noon, Sam Garton called Matt to his freight office. Garton was behind the counter, working on his ledgers, and he lifted his head when Matt approached. There was no sign of humor in his eyes, though usually he had a joke to offer.

136

"Set, Sheriff."

Matt came around the counter and lowered himself into a chair. Garton pushed
back his ledgers and straightened his back,
sighing softly as the kink came out of it.

"It's Saturday," Garton said, "but I'm asking you to take on more trouble." He
rubbed a hand over a three-day stubble on
his jaw. "I got to admit you've made a good
sheriff up to now. I'm for you."

"That leaves only Ezra against me," Matt
commented dryly.

Matt knew by Garton's slow nod what the
man was thinking. Ezra Meecham had won
his round when he insisted that drunks
should be turned loose on sobering up.
Matt had done this for Jake Dill and the six
other men he had arrested since that first
time. It weakened the law, because punish-
ment for a drunk became nothing but a
warm place to sleep and a free meal.

"I ain't worried about Ezra," Sam Garton
said slowly, "but he's got a point. You keep
men in jail, and you got to feed them. You'd
have the jailhouse full of bums waiting out
the winter."

"I agreed to that," Matt admitted. "Otherwise I'd have fought Ezra more."

"But," Garton went on, "having law here
won't run business to Shackville like he

claims. Shackville's too far off. It's nothing but a freight rest and . . ."

When he paused, Matt finished for him, "And a hangout for trail robbers. Get to your trouble, Sam."

"A man can't make no profit, no matter how good his business is, if he don't get goods through. Your paw built a good freight line north and south out of here, and Abe and me kept it rolling. But there's no need of my working if the freight don't get where it's supposed to."

"You're long-winded after a day's work," Matt observed. "There hasn't been a holdup this fall."

"They've waited to see how you'd turn out," Garton said. He laid his thick hands flat on the counter and shook his head. "I did some figuring today. They've been waiting, but now they ain't waiting. Jeremy's train is coming down soon — the last 'til spring, probably."

"How do you know?" Matt asked. "You hire spies, Sam?"

"I figured it out," Garton said again. "They'll want this last shipment, and they'll figure you're too busy with the town."

Matt shrugged. "I can't watch the town and the freight road at the same time," he pointed out.

"Shackville is a snake's nest," Sam Garton said. "Whatever happens here comes from Shackville." He held a pen to the light that came through the window, and he seemed to find something fascinating in the ink-stained tip. "A word of warning ——"

"I don't need warning about Shackville," Matt interrupted. "They robbed enough freights when my father had the business." He rose and went to the door. "I'll ride, but it won't be to do more than warn them, Sam. I have no proof of what they plan to do."

Garton seemed satisfied. Nodding, he said, "Just don't let them do the warning — with lead."

Matt got his sorrel from the livery, ignoring Luther Colban's obvious curiosity, and went home for his slicker. After that, he took the freight highway north. Thinking about the fancy name for the wagon road made Matt smile. It was nothing more than a narrow trail that snaked through the timbered hills into Canada.

Three miles along, Matt put his horse onto a narrow path through timber, climbed a sharp rise, and came out on a sparsely treed bench that was Morgan's northernmost range. This was a shortcut that a man on horseback or afoot could take and save himself hours of following the twistings of the freight road.

Before he reached the boundary of Morgan's graze he saw a rider coming rapidly toward him, and he made out a hand waving for him to stop. He reined in. It was Lucy Morgan, riding her usual man-fashion, coming full tilt on a fast dun pony over the damp uneven ground.

"You'll break your neck someday," was his greeting.

"It's my own," she answered. She was laughing, rain streaming from her face and off her hat. She looked even smaller on horseback than she had at the dance. She kept on laughing. "Why haven't you been up lately, Matt?"

"My job keeps me busy."

"Not that busy," she gibed. "It's that new woman, isn't it? She's very pretty, Matt."

"Now," Matt said easily, "you can't catch me that way, Lucy. I hear you've been seeing Adam Bede."

"One for one." She smiled. "Cole introduced us. Adam's been up for supper."

"And Dave and Pete let a friend of Cole's come?"

"Is he a friend?" she countered quickly. "I understood they had a business deal. Adam wants money to have a printing press freighted in." She shook her head, sending a spray of raindrops spinning from the brim of her hat. "But I didn't stop you to talk about Adam."

"Morgan cows?" Matt asked.

She was sober now, her laughter gone. "We're still losing them — some here, some there. It was a big bunch this week." Clasping her small hands over her saddle horn, she leaned forward. "Oh, Matt! It isn't Cole. Dad and Dave blame everything on him, but it isn't."

"He's pretty busy readying himself for winter," Matt agreed. "I'll see what I can find."

"There's nothing to find," she said. "Our men know these trails better than you, and they've had no luck. I just wanted to tell you because you'll hear talk and think it's Cole."

"I reserve judgment on everything, Lucy," he said.

"Thanks, Matt." She smiled again, a rainwet smile that was warm and soft on her lips. "And bring Miss Winter up some day."

"Call on her when you go to town," he countered. "It isn't improper."

"Improper!" She waved the idea away with a quick flip of her hand, turned, and spurred the dun. Matt watched her out of sight and then put the sorrel into a gentle jog.

Now that he had heard Lucy, Matt concerned himself with the trail underfoot. But there were no unusual signs. Men wise enough to get away consistently with Morgan cattle would be too wise to leave markings easy to read. Past the edge of Morgan land, he looked more to his right and left, and it was not far from the beginning of the rocky treeless ground near the pass leading to the freight road that he spotted something. Going to his left, he reined in by a clump of buckbush.

He sat a moment, studying the tuft of mixed red and white hair that could be nothing but part of a cow's winter coat. The brush was crushed in a wide swath; it was that which had first drawn his attention. Glancing at the sky, he decided he had a few moments to spare, and he followed the trail the beef had made.

It was not easy going, even though the signs were quite fresh. He picked up not only the hoofprints of steers but those of a rider. Shortly he found himself blocked by a hillside that rose steep and sheer and with only a single narrow cut in its face. The rain-soft ground showed clearly where the rider had driven the beef into the cut, and Matt followed.

It was no more than a defile, cut by nature through walls of thick hard rock. In less than a fifth of a mile it broke suddenly into a grassy basin. Matt hauled up, studying the layout spread in front of him. In his days of riding for Morgan's Double M, beef had never been put on this far north range, and so this was new territory to Matt.

In front of him was a cabin with a lean-to shed tacked on the rear, and beside the shed three horses grazed peacefully. Smoke rose from a chimney poking out of the shed roof, and not far behind Matt could see a man working away at the ground.

Before he could make up his mind how to act, a figure appeared in the doorway of the lean-to. By the man's size, Matt recognized Jud Keppel. Lifting a hand, Matt called out and then rode forward. Keppel was lounging in the doorway when Matt came close to him. His big heavy features had no expression on them.

Matt sniffed. "Having a beef fry, Jud?"

"Thought we'd eat," Jud answered in his high voice.

Matt eased himself out of the saddle. Jud made no move. There was a rustling behind him and he said, "Put that gun down, Shorty. It ain't anybody but the sheriff."

Matt took it with a grin. He said, "Nice

little place you've got tucked away here."

"Handy," Jud said. "We found a silver ledge back a ways. Not much pay, but it all helps." He moved aside as Matt showed signs of wanting to go into the lean-to. Matt stepped past, into a dim room thick with greasy smoke that came from beef frying on an ancient stove.

"Smells like Morgan beef," Matt said casually.

"Now," Jud complained, "it ain't, Matt. It's a stray I found. A poor lost maverick. We couldn't do no more'n protect it from the winter."

"So you're salting it down," Matt observed.

"You might say," Jud agreed.

Matt turned for the door. "Mind if I go dig up the hide your friend is burying out there, Jud?"

Jud scratched his head with a heavy finger. "I might ask for a search warrant, Sheriff. But seeing as it's you . . ."

Jud's attitude told Matt what he would find. Jud got the man working with a shovel to uncover what he had just buried so laboriously. It was a rolled-up hide. Stretching it out, Matt studied the carefully blotted brand and flipped over the hide. He grinned and got to his feet.

"I'd say it was a Bar Cross once."

"Could have been," Jud said emotionlessly. "Found it near a herd Jake Dill seems to be feeding. Jake's handy at blotting brands."

Matt glanced toward the west; at the edge of the grassy cup, almost invisible against the hillside, were a few dots that he knew would be the rest of the herd that had been driven in here recently. Shaking his head, Matt returned to his horse.

"I wouldn't know what charge to take you in on, Jud."

"No charge," Jud said. "Even if that cow was Jake's, taking something from him ain't stealing."

Matt looked down at him from the saddle. "Morgan has been losing cows again, Jud."

He saw the first emotion on the big man's face, a clamping together of his lips. "I took sixty Morgan head away from a herd some of Dill's men was driving to the Canada mines," he said shortly. "I put them back where they belonged."

Matt believed him; it was the odd kind of thing Jud Keppel would do. "And let the Bar Cross beef go through?"

Jud was expressionless again. "Them poor Canadians got to eat, too," he said.

Matt reined the sorrel around. "Just

remember, Jud, that if I could find this place, someone else could, too."

"Not everybody gets in here — or out," Jud answered.

Matt saw what he meant as he rode back to the narrow defile. A man was perched up above, out of sight to someone riding in but plainly visible from the little grassy bowl. He sat on a rock, the butt of a rifle sticking out from under a poncho covering his knees. He waved as Matt looked up.

Once back on the main trail, Matt put the sorrel to as fast a pace as he dared. It was steep going once he topped the pass, and only when he reached the freight highway again did he relax enough to think about Jud.

That the man had broken a law was indisputable. But what law? Frankly, he did not know. And, understanding what kind of man Jud Keppel was, Matt felt sure he would be worth more picking Morgan beef out of Jake Dill's herds than he would be eating up town funds in the jailhouse. When he considered the problem from every angle, he realized that it represented a change in his thinking which bothered him.

CHAPTER NINE

Before Matt could reconcile the ways of right and wrong, he reached Shackville. Dusk was closing in, and he reined up, resting his horse and staring down at the cluster of grim buildings. Shackville, the one place on the trail between Gaptown and the mines that was wide enough for a rest stop, was composed of a barnlike structure that housed its store and saloon, a stable and corral, and, a short distance off, a half-dozen shacks for tired freighters to rest in.

It looked innocent enough in the half light, but Matt knew that inside the main building was one of the most worthless people in the Northwest. He seemed to do what Jake Dill said, and so far he had been too clever to get caught. Matt was aware that if there was a chance of his being caught, Bald Leggett was always ready to prove that he was as good as any marksman west or east of the Mississippi River.

Matt turned his horse down the slope and rode onto the rolling circle of prairie, incongruous in this country of heavy timber; Shackville was in the center of the prairie. He put the sorrel in front of the main building, loosened his slicker, and went inside. The front room was big and drafty, stretching the length of the building. A half-dozen men were lined at the bar, and another dozen were playing cards at rough wood tables. Bald Leggett was behind the bar, his huge torso and heavy face showing to advantage, but his thick heavy legs, short to the point of being grotesque, well hidden.

The hum of talk faded. Matt walked up to the bar, nodding to the men who stared silently at him. Bald Leggett moved a little so that he stood directly in front of Matt.

"Drink, Sheriff?" He put emphasis on the last word.

"On duty," Matt said, in refusal. Leggett's eyes were mostly hidden behind rolls and puffs of thick fat, and they were difficult to see into clearly. "Sam Garton asked me to stop in."

Bald Leggett reached behind himself and got a lighted cigar from a cracked saucer. "So?" He gnawed the cigar. "Don't he like the way I run the place?"

His inference was that Matt acted as Sam Garton's errand boy, and a flush crawled up Matt's bony face. He stayed silent until his anger was brushed aside by the humor of the idea that he could let someone like this bait him. He said, "He wants Jeremy Cotter to get his freight through when it comes down."

"So?" Bald Leggett said again. He laid his huge hands on the bar top in a typical gesture of innocence. "I didn't contract to give no armed guards, Sheriff. The freight train shows up; I feed it. That's the only job Garton gave me."

His small hidden eyes met Matt's. Matt said, "You might not have that much if something happens to Cotter. It would make things tough for you."

Bald Leggett's smile was quick and almost lost in his fat. "The money, you mean?"

"Money is hard to come by this far out in the hills."

Leggett took his cigar from his mouth. He studied the gnawed tip. His voice was soft when he spoke. "Tell Garton that it will cost him less to let things stand as they are. Tell him that, Sheriff." He sent a quick look around the room, and his whole expression changed. He spat contemptuously. "Now run out of here. Take your badge and run out."

Matt stood where he was, not even angered. "I'm the law here, Leggett. You might not like it, but I'm the law."

As if by a signal the men at the bar and those at the tables broke into a chorus of guffaws. Matt turned slowly, his hands loose at his sides, and looked at them. "You," he said to a man at the nearest table. "You've been in my jail. You and the man next to you."

Bald Leggett said, "Run out, Sheriff. Run out. Have Garton send a man the next time."

Matt did not even look at him. "I'm law enough to put you back in jail if you ever fight again in Gaptown." He turned. "And I'm law enough to put you in, Leggett, when I'm ready."

Leggett said, "When you're ready," and laughed. "Let me know when you're ready, Sheriff." He walked away, down the bar, to draw a beer for a customer.

"I will," Matt said briefly. He started for the door. His hand on the latch, he turned. "Tell Dill that for his sake and yours, Leggett, he'd better see that the freight goes through."

Leggett said mockingly, "Yes, Sheriff."

Matt went through the door, closing it carefully behind him. He mounted the sorrel but stayed where he was, not turning for home in the quick gathering darkness. Some of the men had followed Leggett's cue, and Matt could hear their mocking laughter. But most, he knew, were not laughing. They would be wondering just how much weight he did carry.

He had got no satisfaction, he realized. On the other hand, he had not lost ground by coming here tonight. Leggett knew where he stood, and so did the others. But, Matt was all too aware, Bald Leggett was not the kind to be frightened by threats — rather, he was the kind who would see just how much there was to Matt's strength. And Matt knew that he did not have the strength of Leggett — not alone.

The wash of rain shut away all sound from Matt as the laughter inside stopped. No one came to the door, and so, finally, he reined the horse about.

The slickness of the ground and the deep darkness in the timber made the shortcut impractical, and it was late when Matt reached Gaptown. Only the lights of the saloons, a soft glow in Sam Garton's office, and another from the city building were visible. Matt rode to the livery, ringing the night bell for the boy. Turning over the sorrel when the boy came out sleepily, Matt went to the freight office. Sam Garton was as he had been, hunched over his ledgers. He raised his head and nodded to Matt.

"You got no satisfaction."

"No," Matt agreed. "Bald Leggett wants tribute." He told what had happened.

"You can't arrest him for words, Matt."

"No, but if the freight wagons don't make it through ——"

"You think this will be proof enough?"

"Proof enough to send a posse to search. When I have to, I'll ride on him. But legally, within the law."

Sam Garton's belly shook in silent laughter. "When you're ready, let me know." He bent to his work again.

Matt went into the rain. A crawling anger at his own helplessness with a man like Leggett was beginning to work like yeast in him. Yet his faith in his way of the law remained strong.

Hunching his shoulders, he crossed the street and plodded to Gail's. There was no light, nor did his knock bring any stirring from inside. Despite the darkness of Gaptown, he knew it was too early for her to have gone to bed.

For some reason she was not at home.

Matt retraced his steps to Main Street. Luther Colban was at the door of his livery stable, prowling as he often did when he couldn't sleep. Matt went up to him.

"Quiet?" Matt asked.

"Quiet enough," Luther said. "Your boy Toby went up the street just now for a last check." His face crinkled with laughter. "Before I went home the first time your new girl came to the office and went inside, and she and Toby came out together."

Matt accepted the teasing with a smile. "No connection at all, Luther." He moved away, following Main southward. He watched for Gail but could not see her. He remembered that she had been at Bee Clancy's before, but the thought of going there to inquire for her went too deeply against him, and he continued on Main past Hill, not turning.

A few men came out of Lamont's as he went by. He ignored them, rounded the corner of the building, and walked to the alley. He followed it up, between the rear of Lamont's and the shacks behind it. He was being foolish, he knew. There were a half-dozen places she could have gone, a half-dozen things she could be doing. But still, she shouldn't be out. It was late at night and raining. As quiet as Gaptown was this night, he didn't care for things as they were.

He found himself by Bee Clancy's, without really being aware of the way he had got there. Before going to the door, he made a circuit around the building. The reluctance that had held him from coming directly here kept his hand from striking the big knocker, but his footsteps must have achieved the same effect, for the door opened. Bee Clancy blocked it with her big blondness.

"Business, Matt?"

"Looking for someone," Matt said.

She was silent a moment while they both listened to the sounds of laughter. Then a dance tune came from inside, followed by the noise of booted feet hitting hard on the wooden floor.

"She isn't here, Matt."

"I didn't expect her to be."

"A man is a man," Bee said. "You came because you didn't expect to find her here. Is it hope or expect that you mean, Matt?"

"One or the other," Matt said. "She wrote a letter once in care of you."

Bee's usually friendly expression turned cold and distant. "What you want to know, Matt, ask of her. What would I know — of a lady like that?" She saw Matt's expression and added, "She has never come inside. That's the truth."

"She needs no defense," Matt said. He waited a moment, then smiled. Though he was worried, he was relieved as well. Bee would not lie; lying was not a part of her. "Thanks," he added, and backed away.

The door closed on him and he went down the alley and into Lamont's by the back way. He saw Toby moving gingerly through the crowd, and he followed.

Toby looked at him without smiling. "I got no drunks yet, Matt."

"Tame," Matt commented. "Let's walk." On the sidewalk they faced south, strolling toward the deserted Chinese laundry. He said, "I hear Gail came into the office."

"To tell me she went to your house and borrowed your thirty-eight."

"I gave her bullets for the derringer," Matt said. "What did she want with the thirty-eight?"

"She didn't say. When I told her you was gone on business, she asked me to walk her home." He turned his sharp little face up to Matt. "Something wrong?"

"She isn't home," Matt said. He let the matter drop.

Toby moved restlessly. "Did you see Jake?"

"No," Matt said. "Bald Leggett was all innocence." He added, "I got no satisfaction."

"You won't get any," Toby said. He sounded uneasy. "I'll check Hewitt's, Matt. You go on back. Maybe she's home by now."

"Yes," Matt agreed. He watched Toby cross the street, stepping lightly in the mud, and then he walked on, turning at the laundry and following the alley back to Bee's again. He went along Hill to Main and down Main again. He peered into every recess, feeling the unreasonableness of his worry but unable to do anything about it. Finally the emptiness of his stomach drove him into Lamont's for bread, salted meat, and coffee. Then he resumed his walking. He made a full round without seeing anyone.

Finally he came to the Chinese laundry again, standing where it backed against the alley. The nearest light came from the upstairs of Lamont's, and it slashed dimly and yellowish through the rain onto the mud at his feet. Moving to see the street, Matt heard the sucking sound of hoofbeats in the mud.

It was Cole Pitman riding away from Lamont's with Texas. He watched them reach the foot of the hill and pause to settle in their saddles before starting up. What brought his glance to the building hulking above him, he did not know. A chance to feel the mist on his face or a hopeful peering for a break in the sky, perhaps. The thought did not stay with him long enough to be remembered. In glancing upward he could see her outlined on the laundry roof. She was standing, leaning over the rickety fire wall. A gleam of light from Lamont's picked up her silhouette and flashed briefly from the gun she held.

He did not call out but ran to the steps at the back of the building, taking them two at a time. He came onto a flat roof, laced with clothesline. Ducking low, he ran toward her. He saw her turn, her face white against the night, and then she spun back, lifting her arm. Matt reached her and hit her with his shoulder, throwing out an arm to catch her and at the same time striking at her raised arm with his wrist. The gun made a loud angry sound as it sent a bullet upward.

"Matt! Matt!" It was not anger but anguish, and he let his arm drop from her waist.

He looked down. Pitman had started his horse up the grade, but the sound had evidently stopped him, and now he and Texas were both facing the town.

"See!" she cried hoarsely. "Do you see him? No fear that any man would touch Cole Pitman!"

"Cole," Matt called down. "Hold up, Cole."

"All right," Pitman said good-naturedly. "Arrest us. It's too wet to ride home, anyway."

Gail stood close to Matt, and once more he put his arm around her. He could feel her trembling, and he knew that she was sobbing, though the sounds were muffled inside her.

"We'll go down," he said softly. "He can't tell who you are."

"You did," she said. She turned away.

He came to the head of the stairs right behind her. "I could tell," he said, "because I can see you with my eyes shut."

She turned, her face very close. "Finally you make love to me — after you find me breaking your law."

"Give me the gun and go home," he said. "I'll come soon."

She thought, I felt like a waiting wife once tonight. Now I'm ordered about like one. "All right," she said.

"I'm hungry," Matt told her, thinking that it might give her something to do, something to occupy her mind until he arrived. He helped her down the steps and stayed where he was until she had disappeared around the corner of the building. He took the opposite direction, going to meet Cole Pitman. They were still waiting for him.

"Let Texas ride on," Matt said.

"Go on, Texas," Pitman said. "Did you shoot at me, Matt?" His voice was pleasant. He seemed content with himself.

Texas Zinker rode a short distance up the hill and then reined in.

Matt said, "I didn't do the shooting, but you were the target."

"Tell her," Pitman said, "to do better next time." He laughed. "Tell her to pick a time when you aren't likely to be around."

"There's no reason for joking," Matt said stiffly. "And there won't be a next time. I'm the law here, Cole."

Cole Pitman laughed again, wholeheartedly. "You do all the shooting from now on, is that it?"

"Keep away from her," Matt said, ignoring his humor.

"So she told you?"

"No," Matt answered. "But if you hadn't been bothering her, she wouldn't have tried to shoot you. If she had wanted to shoot you from the start, she would have done it long ago. Keep away."

"When you want a job," Pitman said, "I'll give it to you." He laughed again. "Any man who reasons like that should be working for me." Touching spurs to his horse, he rode up the hill. Texas fell in beside him, and shortly they were out of Matt's sight.

Matt turned in the rain and walked toward Gail's house. There was a light now, and warmth flooded him when she opened the door. He went into the kitchen, where he dropped his slicker and hat. Wiping his boots with a rag that she provided, he went to the pump at the sink and washed his hands. He could smell coffee and the food that she was cooking. Done with his cleaning, he looked at her. She was not smiling.

"I was abrupt," he said. "I wanted your anger turned away from him."

"I know," she said. "Why did you stop me?"

"It's my job."

She set the table, working but not looking at him. He admired her grace, the quiet beauty of her under the soft lamplight. Even with the faint signs of tears still fresh on her cheeks, she was beautiful. The wall of reserve that he felt around her, he took as a matter of course. He had not expected her to be as free with him as she had been. He took a chair and waited for her to speak.

"You're so serious in your job," she said. "You really feel that you stand for justice?"

"I try to," he said stiffly. "Justice isn't a thing to ridicule." He pushed his chair against the wall and rolled a cigarette.

"What is justice?" she demanded suddenly. "Waiting for a man to make a mistake and get arrested? Cole Pitman will die of old age before you catch him that way. He'll cheat you if you wait, Matt."

Matt was still for a moment. When he

spoke he chose his words carefully. "Tonight I admitted I love you."

"You took an odd way of telling me," she remarked. She bent to the stove, not looking at him.

"And," he went on, "I wouldn't want you to have to hide because it was your bullet that killed a man. I wouldn't want you to have to go away from here."

She turned her heat-flushed face toward him. There was humor in her gray eyes and on her quietly smiling lips. "How long I've waited to hear you say that — and you have to do it with a broken law between us!"

She straightened, moving her hand in a short sharp gesture. "It's your law, Matt. Pick it up!"

He walked to her, dropping his cigarette into the stove. He put his hands on her shoulders and looked down into her face. "There are only two reasons for you to feel that Cole Pitman needs killing — either he killed before and you're taking an eye for an eye, or he came here by force this evening."

"Neither one," she said.

"Yet you came here and you waited and you tried to kill him."

"I'll try again," she said flatly. "I wasn't sure that I would kill him until tonight. I'll try again." She had lost her faint smile, and her eyes were grave. He could feel the tenseness of her body beneath his fingers. And suddenly the tension was gone, and she began to tremble.

He drew her gently toward him. When she did not lower her head, he kissed her on the mouth. She raised her arms and pressed her hands against his back, holding him.

Then she pulled herself away abruptly. "The potatoes are scorching!" Attending to them, she faced him again. "You would make love to a woman who swears to break your laws!"

"You won't," Matt said quietly.

She ignored him and spoke in a low voice. "Six years ago my cousin went away with Cole Pitman. We lived in Denver. We were raised together by my aunt. Have you a close brother or sister?"

"No," he said. "You don't need to tell it."

She said, "While my aunt and I waited for word, my aunt died. Her mother, you understand. There was no word at all, and she just sickened and died. It may not be the reason — she was old. But she did die with no word from Ellen."

She was putting food on the table as she talked. "There was some money, and I used a lot of it to find her. But I couldn't. Then, last summer, I had a letter. The only letter.

Ellen was ill. Until she became frightened of dying she wouldn't write. Pride."

"She didn't come here with Cole?"

"No," she said. She poured coffee. "Come and eat now. Cole left her in Wyoming. Three years ago she found out where he was, and she followed."

"And went to Bee Clancy's?"

Her voice was low and bitter. "It was the same sort of thing that Cole left her to in Wyoming. What else was there for her?"

"She caused no gossip?"

"She wasn't that kind. She was a mouse. Bee Clancy told me that night in the alley that she kept a gun under her pillow, and every night she prayed she would have courage enough to use it if he came. He never did. She waited, but he never came near her."

"You speak in the past," Matt said wonderingly.

"While you were away this summer, Cole had her sent out. He saw that she got to Spokane Falls and onto a stagecoach. With some money, of course. After I came, Bee Clancy told me that she had had a letter — from a friend on the coast." Her voice broke sharply. Catching it, she went on in the same quiet tone, "The letter was to ask what should be done with Ellen's effects."

"Ah," Matt said. "Cole learned of it. He came here tonight to find out how much you were going to tell?"

"Yes." She sat silently, watching him eat, taking only coffee for herself. "And then I went to kill him. I lay on that roof for hours. Some night I'll have more luck."

"He'll hang himself if you wait," Matt said. "His own injustice will seek him out."

She shook her head at him, but she made no answer. When he was through eating he rose from the table and they went into her parlor. He sat smoking, looking at her; neither of them spoke.

"There'll be war here," he said finally. "You can feel it building up. Things have been too quiet these past days. Men are walking too softly. Cole Pitman isn't satisfied with what he has, and the Morgans aren't men to let Pitman keep what he's taken already. They'll make Gaptown their battleground when the time comes."

He finished his cigarette and immediately rolled another. "Jake Dill will be in on it. He's already behind Shackville. They challenged me tonight — and for tonight they've won."

"You're in danger?"

"There's always danger in enforcing the law. All work is dangerous here. A man can

164

lose his life any morning out on the range or in the woods or stoping a mine. But no one is after my life just because it's mine; they want to kill what I stand for." He nodded half to himself. "I can't ask you to marry me until this danger is over."

"Is that a law of yours, too?" she smiled quizzically.

"My law is fairness," he said. "Because I go by it doesn't mean that I created it. Fairness to all men and one to another, so that both will have an equal chance to live and die in peace."

She came and sat beside him, putting a hand on his arm. "Your belief is too strong, Matt. It will hurt you."

He inclined his head toward her, kissing her briefly. Then he rose. "They want to break me. I've not much power yet, but already I've bothered them — like a fly on a horse's hide. They'll try to break me."

"How do you know?"

He looked worriedly down at her. "After tonight, I think that they'll try to rob Jeremy Cotter's freight train. Even if they hadn't thought of it before, they'll try to rob it now just to draw me out."

"And you'll go?"

His look was one of surprise. "I'll go," he said. "The job of the law is to protect."

She said quietly, "After the injury is done. Why couldn't you go out and arrest Jake Dill now?"

"I have no proof."

She shook her head slowly back and forth. "No proof — and after all the things he has done. But you have proof against me, and I'm not arrested."

"You're in protective custody," he said dryly. "If you try to shoot Cole again I'll consider it a breach of faith and put you in jail."

"In jail? Until when?"

"Until such time as we can get a court here," he said, and turned toward the door.

She watched him go. "I believe you would," she said, half to herself. "I really believe that you would."

And maybe he should, she thought, for his own sake. She had heard the gossip — unfounded as much Gaptown gossip was — concerning herself and Matt. Daisy had brought it up, as a friend giving warning, and Gail's only answer had been, "He takes his meals with me. That is all."

Now, though, the gossip worried her. If the story about what she had done got about, it would be one more thing against Matt. To many, the fact that he had not arrested her would be proof that they were more than just friends.

She said aloud, "And his law is too weak already."

Chapter Ten

The first part of the following week, a rider from the Canadian mines brought the news that the freight outfit had started south. The information crystallized a problem of Matt's into an answer. The truth in Gail's words that the law waited until injury was done galled him, and he decided to ride with Jeremy Cotter. His hope was to prevent the robbery that he was almost sure would come.

Telling Toby to take over, he rode for the Canadian border. By going within a mile of Shackville and then over a saddle in the mountains, he could come onto the freight highway just south of Canada without being seen by Bald Leggett. He had made the trip often enough with his father to be able to judge the time Jeremy Cotter should arrive at the border.

He was within four hours of guessing the time right and, just before dusk, he picked up the freight train. Jeremy Cotter showed no surprise at seeing him.

"Figuring on something happening, Matt?"

Matt glanced back along the line of heavily laden wagons. "This'll be your last trip out for the winter," he said. "And it looks like you're loaded."

"Yes," Jeremy Cotter admitted. He squinted ahead into the gathering winter darkness. "It smells like snow. I'll be lucky if I make it out of Gaptown this year."

"You have to," Matt said dryly. "I hear Adam Bede is having a printing press shipped in. We can spend the winter reading."

Jeremy Cotter laughed at the thought of Gaptown reading. As driver of the lead wagon, he continued to peer forward, seeking the way. "Broken axle slowed us back there," he grumbled. "Now it's coming dark, and we ought to be by Shackville."

They started a low rise that, once topped, would give them a final easy grade into Shackville. Here the forest was heavy, and branches from the dark firs brushed against the wagons and tried to sweep the men's hats from their heads. It was a bad spot, for, though the mules seldom spooked, some of the horses ridden by the guards would turn skittish. This would occasionally cause the mules to stop and wait until such foolishness ceased.

Jeremy's growl over the broken axle was cut off abruptly. A gun burst raked the night and a bullet spatted into the side of the lead wagon. A sharp volley of shots followed, pinging viciously off the ore piled on the wagons. Jeremy jerked the reins, cursing angrily. Matt swung his horse aside and pulled his forty-four free.

He had no time for anything else. The attack was not the kind that man could see and ward off. Nor was it where Matt had expected. He had not thought they would be foolish enough to make their try this close to Shackville. He heard the boiling of horses and the shrill swearing of men. A last volley of shots burst from the thick forest, and Matt felt the hot stabbing fire of lead catch him and lift him out of the saddle as if he had been so much dust. There was the feel of cool clammy mud striking his face. He had a vague remembrance of trying to fight to his feet, to get his gun around to where he could use it, and that was all.

In the upstairs sitting room at Bill Lamont's, Cole Pitman listened to Jake Dill make his boast.

"That's the way of it," Dill said. He drained off his glass of whiskey and leaned back with a satisfied sigh.

"I didn't order you to get Ross," Pitman said irritably. He fingered his own glass, undecided whether he liked this turn of events or not. It had been over a week now since Jeremy Cotter's weary crew had staggered half frozen into Gaptown, packing Matt Ross in an old rig they had got at Shackville. The town had buzzed for a while, nor had it quieted completely even yet. But the sluggishness of winter kept some of them from being as riled as they might have been in another season.

"I didn't expect to find him riding with the freighters," Dill said in a slightly hurt voice. "But since he was fool enough to do it, I wasn't going to pass up the chance."

Pitman said, "The only reason some of the town hasn't got up a posse to run you out is because Ross is still alive."

Jake Dill grinned, showing his broken teeth. "Me? How in hell can they prove it was me?"

Pitman took time to light a cigar. He said contemptuously, "Proof? What makes you think a posse'd need proof? When a mob gets an idea, it doesn't act like Ross — it doesn't wait for proof. It moves first and thinks later."

"There's nothing they could do to me,"

Dill insisted. He poured himself another shot of whiskey. Pitman watched him, aware that Dill's hand was steady. Whatever else he might think of the man, he had to admit Dill was no coward.

But he said, "I notice you haven't let yourself be seen in town lately. And you'd be smart to stay out of sight a while longer."

"I intend to," Dill answered. "I got too much work to do." His grin came again. "Me and the boys struck it pretty rich, Pitman. We found a pocket of high-grade ore to work."

Pitman brushed the humor aside with a wave of his cigar. "Nevertheless, Dill," he said flatly, "I want no more action taken against Ross until I say it's time. The town is stirred up too much. Let them simmer down. Let the winter make them soft."

"I got a score to settle with Ross. I ain't done with him."

"You're done until I tell you to start again!"

Dill lowered his whiskey glass and stared into Pitman's cold dark eyes. They sat like that for a long full minute, neither man speaking, neither man giving ground. Then, reluctantly, Dill's eyes slid to one side, and he picked up his glass again. He drained it with a sullen defiant motion.

Pitman said, "Don't think that your whiskey-soaked bully-ragging miners are worth so much, Dill. I picked my men for a purpose, remember. They don't get their wages just because they can herd beef."

"All right," Dill said.

Pitman stood up. "Keep out of town. Keep away from Ross. Go work your mine for a while. I'll tell you when the time is right."

"Be sure it ain't too long, that's all," Dill grumbled.

"It won't be too long," Pitman assured him. "No longer than it takes the town to go back to sleep." It was the town's reaction that bothered him. When he took over he wanted to be too strong to be pushed around. He wanted to be in before they woke up to what was happening. After that he wouldn't care what they thought or did. Once he was set firmly in the saddle, men like Abe Parkis could knuckle under or get out.

"Now get back to your hills," he said, "and stay there."

Matt did not remember the day when he first opened his eyes and saw the familiar pattern of his own sitting-room walls. Time closed in on him again. Once he roused, clear-headed enough to recognize Abe Parkis. He asked for Jeremy Cotter.

"Got through," Abe said in his rusty voice. "One man got scratched besides you." His tone was bitter. "They took the teams, wagons, and all. They left Jeremy and the bunch to walk in. Morgan found the teams and wagons south of town not long ago."

Matt understood. Jake Dill would have a lot of "high-grade ore" to take from his mine bit by bit during the long winter. He smiled ruefully, started to answer, and then darkness came on him again.

The snow that came during this time chinooked off only once and then stayed. After two months Matt still lay in bed, but he was sitting up now, clear-headed and able to see the snow-covered yard in front of his house. It piled deeper and deeper until, in February, it stopped and settled down to a biting freeze that drove everything to cover.

Abe had brought a doctor in from Spokane Falls, at the very first, and had kept him there at heavy expense until Matt was on the mend. On his last visit the doctor complimented Gail and Adam Bede on their fine job of nursing.

"You fixed it so he may get around by the first spring thaw," he told Adam Bede, the first day Matt was able to sit up.

To Matt, he said, "You'll carry lead for the rest of your life. It'll hurt sometimes in cold weather, but you can stand that."

Adam Bede, who had watched and practiced until Abe claimed he was as smart as the doctor, said, "How will I know when he's ready to walk?"

The doctor peered at Adam. "Young man, stand him up and let him take a step. If he falls over, put him back to bed. Good day, sir."

That was the last they saw of him. Jeremy Cotter had got back to Gaptown before the deepest snow, and two of his men, tired of doing nothing, had offered to sled the doctor out. Abe said ruefully that he had never seen such a little man eat so much.

Adam Bede seemed pleased at the doctor's going and began to care for Matt in earnest. Matt, when he managed to generate interest, was surprised at the change in Bede. He had toned down his flamboyant clothing, finding it impractical for winter wear. Instead he wore a pair of scuffed high boots, a clean but plain shirt, and a cowhide vest. When he went out he threw over this a buffalo coat he had won at cards and added a huge hat that was black with a wide soft brim. He reminded Matt of a painting he had once seen of a British stagecoach robber. To compensate for the loss of his fine clothes, Bede had grown a thick luxurious brown beard, and he looked at this in the mirror whenever he had the chance.

"Adam," Matt said, on the day that things mattered again to him, "tell me the truth of it."

Adam Bede stroked his beard happily. "Toby has kept the laws. So you've proved your choice of deputy. Of course everyone knows that they're lying quietly until the snow goes."

"By then I'll be up," Matt said. "And what about you?"

"Ah," Adam Bede said. "My press has come from the coast. Jeremy's men sledded it in for want of something to do." He nodded in self-satisfaction. "Inside of two weeks I'll put the first Gaptown paper on the streets. No longer will I deal cards, my friend, but words. Strong words."

Matt frowned. "Didn't Cole Pitman lend you the money for that press?"

Bede's smile was plain through his heavy beard. "Most of it."

"Then," Matt reasoned, "he'll expect you to help him control Gaptown."

Bede shut his eyes. "He is expecting — yes." He opened his eyes and looked steadily at Matt. "I gave him my note with the press

175

as security. I paid the freight myself, and there is money enough on deposit at the bank to pay the freight back. If I can't meet my debt Pitman won't lose anything. He can sell the press on the coast with no loss."

"Meaning?" Matt queried.

"Meaning that I'm an honest dealer," Adam Bede told him.

Matt flexed his fingers and found them strong enough to roll a cigarette. He did so. "Who are you figuring on dealing out?"

Bede came forward with a match when the cigarette was finished. "Ezra Meecham for one," he said. "And I'll deal Gail in."

Matt remembered dim visions of Gail, tall and cool, moving about his bedside. He said, "Abe told me she had lost her school job. I thought I was dreaming it."

"No dream," Bede said briefly. "Ezra forced her to resign."

"On what complaint?"

"On the complaint that it is not fitting for a schoolteacher to lie on the laundry roof and shoot at one of our more substantial citizens."

Matt blew a luxurious stream of smoke from his nostrils and shifted his weight a little. "She didn't admit that?"

"No. There was a witness. Jake Dill." Bede drew up a chair and lowered himself into it.

"Recently Dill has been coming back to town."

"Dill didn't see it," Matt said quietly.

"Most people know it's a lie," Adam said. "But they aren't doing anything about it." His face flushed a little and he threw out an arm to emphasize his words. "They think he shot you, too, but they aren't doing anything about that. That's another thing I'm putting in my paper. A would-be murderer goes free while the sheriff lies at the point of death. He flaunts himself, and they sit and look at him!"

"You sound like an editorial I read once," Matt said dryly. "Adam, if you condemn one man for attempted murder you have to condemn a hundred. This is raw country. And who would you have arrest Jake — Toby?"

"Not Toby, but there are others."

"Those others appointed me the law and they'll let me be the law," Matt said. "I'll soon be up, and then I'll ride. I warned Shackville once. This time I'll do something about it."

Adam Bede's expression showed his approval. He saw Matt's head fall back wearily and he rose, taking the cigarette from Matt's fingers. He said, "Lucy Morgan and her brother have been visitors. Miss Lucy seems quite concerned."

Matt's grin was faint. "Concerned for me or you, Adam?"

"Why, now," Adam Bede said, "I forgot to ask her." He added after a moment, "She's still seeing Cole Pitman. She's trying to keep the peace between Double M and Bar Cross."

You hope it's only that, Matt thought. He said, "Someone is coming."

Adam looked briefly through the window. "Gail. To cook your supper. I'll be going."

"Does she know I've recovered?"

"No. Why else would I be leaving?"

Matt watched Adam's departing back. "I can count on him," he murmured.

And, he knew, he would soon need men that he could count on.

When Matt had recuperated enough to take a few tentative steps around his sitting room, Adam Bede allowed him to have more visitors. At Matt's request, Abe Parkis came, bringing with him Luther Colban and Sam Garton. Adam was already there, hovering like a hen over his patient.

Matt came directly to the point. "I'll soon be ready to ride, and I want to form a committee."

Without a need for words, they all knew

what he meant. One by one, they nodded agreement.

"The five of us will be enough," Matt said. "And unless Shackville spies get ahead of us, we'll clean the nest out." His voice roughened with remembrance. "Once Jake Dill is in prison, Cole Pitman will have less to count on."

"Your brain is still fevered," Abe observed, "if you think Cole needs Jake. Jud Keppel and his sniping at Bar Cross beef is of more value to Morgan than Dill is to Pitman."

"We'll see," Matt said. "Toby will stay here. I can't ask a man to ride on his own father."

"No more than you can ask the saloon owners who count on Dill and Pitman for their living," Adam Bede said.

Matt nodded. "This will be enough," he said, looking around. His eyes met the gaze of first one man and then another. It occurred to him that he should state his position. "This is a lawful posse," he warned. "Every man here is to be deputized. There is to be no killing or shooting unless we're attacked."

"I say, ride them down and burn them out," Luther Colban demanded angrily. "Shackville is a running sore."

"We aren't after Shackville itself," Matt

said. "It is a good thing to have — as a freight rest. I want to clean it up, not burn it down."

"To warn them again?" Sam Garton asked heavily.

Matt shook his head. "They had their warning." He stopped long enough to shape and light a cigarette. Then he said, "Remember, we want Jake Dill. The warrant is against him."

"Will they wait while we serve a warrant?" Sam Garton demanded. "They'll meet us with guns or a trap. The law is too slow."

"I'd arrest a man here if he attacked first," Matt said briefly. "The law is useless unless it's lawful."

"You're right," Abe Parkis agreed. "But sometimes the law is useless, anyway. I'm agreeing with Luther and Sam."

"I follow Matt," Adam Bede said soberly. "It's his law — and he's the one carrying Jake Dill's lead."

Matt studied them again. "It's three to two," he said. "But I can't accept your way. If you decide against me, I'll turn in my badge and we'll go as vigilantes. If we ride as I say, we ride lawfully."

"Force is all they know," Luther Colban said. "Law by force is all they'll ever understand. I agree that we need Shackville — a clean Shackville. All right, clean it up by building on its ashes."

Adam Bede looked worriedly at Matt. "We can decide this later. When Matt is up and around more, we ——"

"No," Matt said. "We can decide it now. You men here have always spoken for the rest of the businessmen. Do so now."

After a moment, Garton said, "We hired you. We'll go along with you." But his concession was reluctant.

Abe Parkis made a dry chuckling sound of agreement. "You can see we want our money's worth out of your salary, Matt." He got up. "Let us know when we ride."

Chapter Eleven

Before long, Matt tested himself with a short horseback ride. He found that the thaws and freezes had left the trails thinly covered with snow but hard and slick. To wait too much longer would mean plowing through clinging and hampering mud. He rode back to town and went to Abe Parkis.

"I'm ready to ride," Matt told him.

"All right," Abe agreed. "I'll tell the others."

"Keep it quiet if we can," Matt warned.

"If we can," Abe said dourly. "At dusk?"

"At dusk," Matt said, and left.

Shortly before the time to go, Matt got his horse and rode to Gail's. Though it was still light outside, she had need of a lamp. He could see its glow through the window. He knocked.

She opened the door. Standing there, framed in the lamplight, she looked to him as lovely and golden as it was possible for a woman to be. He stepped inside and shut the door. Taking his hands, she drew him to her, and they kissed gently.

"You're ready to go?"

"Yes." He moved restlessly away. She went into the kitchen and he followed, rolling a cigarette.

"I've fixed an early supper."

"A light one," he requested. "I have to ride fast tonight." He sat at the table while she dished out beans and bread and coffee for him. "You're worried."

She smiled slowly. "Should I be happy to sit and see my man ride into the night — bent on killing?"

"Your man," he repeated. "It will bring me back; I like the sound of it." He bent to his food. "There may be killing. Bald Leggett might not want to give Jake Dill up without a fight. And I doubt if we can hide our coming. There are too many in this

182

town who want to see the law defeated. Someone will go with a warning."

"Is that the law, to attack them without proof?"

Matt smiled slowly at her obvious argument. "I'm not attacking," he explained. "I'm looking for Jake Dill. Abe Parkis swore out a warrant against him — attempted murder. One of Jeremy Cotter's men said that he saw Jake the night I was shot."

"And you believe it?"

Matt rolled a second cigarette and leaned back to enjoy his coffee. "What I believe has nothing to do with it. As the law I have to follow up the complaint." He smoked a few moments in silence, and then asked a question that had weighed on his mind for some time.

"Did Cole come while I was in bed?"

"No, or I would have shot him," she said frankly.

"You won't shoot him unless he comes here, then?"

Her mouth pulled to a thin line. "I held that reservation while you were down. Now that you're up and about, Matt, you can defend your law again. I'll shoot him at the first chance — anywhere."

He sighed gently. "That still stands between us."

183

"Why?" she cried. "Isn't my justice as good as yours? Can't I swear a complaint to myself on Cole Pitman as Abe has done on Jake Dill? Why can't you let me do to Cole what you're planning to do to Shackville? Why am I breaking the law when you're not?"

"It's the way I see things," Matt said. Standing, he smiled down at her. "Since it hasn't happened yet, let's not talk about it."

"You're so blind," she said violently. "Because you can't see it, because you have no — no legal proof, it doesn't exist."

He walked in silence to the other room, scooping his hat from the sofa as he went by. At the door she caught up with him. Her reserve broke, and with a soft cry she flung herself into his arms.

"I won't — tonight. I'll stay and keep the fire up for you."

"Now I can ride easy," he murmured.

When he was ready to go, he held her away from him and opened the door. "Toby'll be on watch," he said. "It isn't likely that Cole will come, but he may have heard we're going."

"If it's to his advantage to know it, he will," Gail said. She gave him a brief kiss and shut the door.

Matt went slowly to his horse, mounted,

and rode into the thickening dusk. It was almost full dark when he pulled into the small group that was waiting a mile west on the highway. They were all there, impatient, their horses stamping and blowing in the cold.

Abe said, chattering, "Swear us in, Matt."

The formalities were quickly over. Matt turned his sorrel and led them down the highway. It was a cold clear night with no moon, and they made definite outlines against the whiteness of the snow on the road. Hoofs squeaked against the slick footing, and here and there ice slowed them beyond their already cautious pace.

The trip was long, but when they pulled in at the crest of the last rise Shackville was brightly lighted below them.

There was no sound but the snapping of trees under the impact of the cold. Matt raised an arm and they eased down the slope. The dark shadow of a man on horseback appeared on the snow behind Bald Legget's saloon building.

"Cut him off," Matt ordered sharply, and Luther Colban swung to his right.

Matt and the others drew up before the saloon. The front door was shut, but light and noise poured from two small windows.

Matt dismounted and looked up at the three men.

"That man running away shows that they know we're here, and why. There may be a trap set."

"If it was Dill," Adam Bede said, "he ran because Pitman told him not to fight yet."

"If it was Dill we should all be after him," Abe Parkis said.

"It's too cold to argue," Sam Garton answered. "Even Shackville is warm inside."

Matt led them to the door and they went in. Just as before, the rush of noise dwindled and ceased at his entrance. Matt stood just inside the doorway, searching the room with his eyes. He saw a scattering of men from Gaptown saloons. Bald Leggett was a formidable bulk behind the bar. Jake Dill was not in sight.

"I came for Dill," Matt said to Leggett.

"I'm not his nurse, Sheriff," Bald Leggett said, with exaggerated politeness in his tone. "And I don't want your kind in here." He looked unblinkingly at the four, who stood with their guns ready.

Matt's anger climbed. "I can arrest you for obstructing justice. You and a few others."

Bald Leggett was still, incredulity moving like a shadow across his huge face. Then he

186

opened his mouth and laughed. Other men in the room took up the sound, and it beat against Matt and his crew from three sides.

Matt was silent. Bald Leggett stopped laughing. "He's arresting us!" he boomed out. "Me and how many of the boys, Sheriff?"

"I'll take them all and sort them out later," Matt said. "Line up, all of you."

There were over a dozen men in the room, and they came to their feet. Those who had been sitting and those at the bar moved aside, leaving a wide lane between Matt and Leggett. A man at the far end of the bar made a move. No one could say that he had gone for his gun, but no one could deny it.

Abe Parkis was the one to shoot. The acrid smell of powder filled the room, and the man screamed, his gun clattering to the floor. "In the hand," Abe said disgustedly.

"Put your hands up where we can see them," Matt said. He turned his head from the direction of the wounded man back to Bald Leggett. Now there was a shotgun lying on the bar, the muzzle pointed toward the group at the door. Bald held it.

"You got to take us," he challenged. There was no movement of his huge body, no expression on his gross face. He was still and white and very cold-looking. All signs of laughter had left him.

"Come peaceable or dead," Sam Garton said.

Matt spoke so that only the men by him could hear. "We haven't the strength to do this. Nor the legal right."

Abe Parkis murmured, "You spoke of obstructing justice."

"My bluff right now," Matt said wearily. "Leggett is right — he isn't Dill's nurse." He stood motionless, bitter, feeling his defeat.

He lifted his voice. "You'll get out of the country, Leggett."

Adam Bede opened the door slowly. Bald Leggett lifted a warning hand as a man in the crowd moved. "No," he said. His voice boomed out, amused again. "Good night, gentlemen." They heard his words as they filed out. "This law is a joke. Let it blow, men."

Adam led the others back into the snow. Mounted again, they faced Matt. Abe Parkis spoke up. "Where did we get? The law ain't even got dignity now. No force, no power. They'll laugh it out of Gaptown."

Matt felt the bitterness more strongly as he saw that even Adam doubted him. "They've had their warning," was all that he could say.

"Warning," Adam Bede agreed. "But tonight it's we who run."

Luther Colban joined the retreating group at the top of the first rise out of Shackville. His horse's head dropped with weariness, its forelegs spraddled.

"Lost him in the brush over east," Colban said. He looked from one to the other. "So you lost."

"For now," Matt agreed. "It was Dill you chased?"

"I'd swear to it. He looked like he was heading for his mine back of Pitman's."

"He isn't afraid," Matt said softly, "or we wouldn't ride home." To the men, he ordered, "Ride on. I came for Dill and I'll go after him." Turning, he put his horse down the grade until he came to where Luther's horse had made tracks through almost belly-deep snow. Hoofbeats came from behind; he was not surprised when Adam Bede pulled up level with him.

"Go tend to your paper, Adam."

"Eye-witness reporting is always the best," Adam Bede said.

Matt rode silently, with Adam Bede just behind him. The snow here was deep, but, as Luther Colban had broken trail, the going was not too bad. Matt said, "Here's

189

where he cut Dill's trail." A little distance on they came to a thicket and spent some time riding around it before they picked up the sign of both men again. Finally they reached a bald spot on a hilltop. Twisting winds reached this place, sweeping it clean of snow. Luther Colban's tracks ended there, turning and following the trail back.

"He lost Dill," Matt said. He kept on, going up the bare ridge that connected this hill to another, and then dropping to the snow-covered lee of a third slope. A late thin moon was up now, giving them light enough with which to pick their way. After a wide circling, Matt found the sign of Dill's horse again. They rode in silence, not trying to push their animals but not trying to hold them back, either.

"We're about level with Gaptown now," Matt said once.

The going grew slower. A wind sprang up, knifing through their clothing whenever they had to ride the crests of the hills. But the timber was thin enough to have let the winds blow away the snow, and so the going was somewhat easier. Always they bore south and a bit east. When the late winter dawn came, the depth of frost came with it, and Matt awoke to the realization that he was growing stiff in the saddle.

190

"Walk and lead awhile," he suggested.

It was somewhat warming, even though the snow went over the tops of their boots and melted against their feet. Matt could feel the weariness creeping over him and the place where he carried Jake Dill's lead began to ache and then to throb with a steady relentlessness. He stumbled once, and Adam Bede stopped to help him back on his horse.

With the dawn a bank of clouds scudded over on a high wind. A snowflake twisted down out of the sullen sky. "We'll lose his tracks, sure," Adam Bede said. "But it's warming up, at least."

"Some consolation," Matt said, through obvious pain. "But we don't need tracks now. Jake didn't turn up that last canyon. This is Pitman's trail we're on now."

Adam Bede laughed with his face stiff and drawn. "In that case we should be at Pitman's in time for coffee."

Snow was coming down thin and fine when they rode into the Bar Cross yard. Pitman came out onto his wide veranda and stared down at them. His house was a fine one, broad and rambling, its peeled log exterior looking too rich for the rawness that surrounded it. The snow-covered mountains rose tier on tier as a backdrop, and in front of him Pitman could look across the valley at Morgan land and Morgan beef whenever he wished.

Matt stayed on his horse when Pitman said, "Come and eat."

"This is no pleasure call," Matt answered. "I want Jake Dill."

Adam Bede sat quietly, his smile small as he watched Cole Pitman. Matt could not help wondering what Pitman would think of Bede being in company with the sheriff.

"Why tell me about Dill?" Pitman demanded equably.

"We trailed him here," Matt said.

"If I had him, I wouldn't admit it," Pitman answered. "And you can't search a man's castle, law or no law." His voice was without anger as he leaned toward them. "There must be a refuge for a man some place."

"I'll remember that," Matt said. "And give Jake this message. He's to be out of this country tonight, or he'll be shot on sight." He pulled the sorrel around and started away.

Adam Bede lingered as Pitman spoke his name questioningly. He said, "What I see and hear I put in my paper, Cole."

"That makes your stand clear enough," Pitman said. He did not sound overly surprised. "I can't argue with your idea of what is fit to put in a paper — but I can object to it."

"Do so personally, then," Adam Bede said amiably. Tipping his hat, he spurred after Matt.

Pitman stood a moment on the porch, letting the snow slant in across the railing and rest whitely on his arms and shoulders. His hands gripped down on the log railing until cold forced him to realize that he was growing numb. He turned then and went into the warmth of the house.

He found Jake Dill in the kitchen, eating and sucking noisily at a cup of coffee. He got a cup for himself, filling it from the big pot on the back of the range. Dill grinned at him but made no other move.

"You fool," Pitman said wearily. "Letting them trail you here!"

"It takes an Indian to hide tracks in the snow," Dill said reasonably. "And what are the odds?"

"Letting them know you'd come to me. Why didn't you stay back with Leggett?"

Jake Dill set down his cup and reached for his tobacco. "They came to arrest me," he pointed out. "I could have stayed and fought. Bald would have helped me, sure."

193

He nodded. "He'd like to cut loose on Ross. But you said it wasn't time yet. You said that yourself."

"I expect a man to use his head — if he has one."

Dill flushed under the insult. "By damn, Pitman! I'm throwing in with you, not hiring out to you. Remember that."

Pitman stood there, watching Dill and waiting. Normally Jake Dill's assumption of equality would have been amusing; now it angered him. Texas Zinker chose that moment to call him to the room where he took his meals. Pitman went in and sat at his place.

"Keep your patience," Zinker warned. "This is still winter."

"I'm sick of patience," Pitman snapped at him. "That's what they're waiting for — the end of winter. They know we'll hit them in the spring. The word's all over town."

"I've heard the reports," Zinker said. He looked closely at Pitman. "Did you lose that newspaperman, Captain?"

Pitman's voice went up in angry impatience. "He's a fool."

Zinker smiled. "He's made fools of us," he corrected. "And you can't touch him until the note falls due."

Pitman slapped the gun riding on his hip.

"I can touch him."

"You need the town," Zinker warned. "You may want their support sometime. You won't get it by killing men like Bede. Let Meecham force him out — or force him over to us."

"He's only one," Pitman said. His irritation was still high, spurring him. "Here's the sheriff and the rest of them that call their interference by the name of law." He stared out the window at the mistily falling snow. "Why else would a man come to a country like this but to get rid of interference?"

"To make his fortune with patience," Zinker said. "And you won't do it this way. Having Meecham force the Winter woman out of her school wasn't smart."

"I want her out of the country," Pitman said roughly.

"If she'd wanted to tell her story she could have done it before this," Zinker pointed out to him. "You're forcing her into defending herself." He waited while Pitman took a gulp of coffee. "I heard a rumor that Bede is circulating a petition to get her reinstated. That will test Ezra Meecham's strength."

Pitman sat rigidly until some of his anger began to simmer down to where he could control it. He said, "Lots of men are swayed

195

by the weight of public opinion. See that the results of the petition tell what we want."

"That's a lot to ask," Zinker pointed out reasonably. "Bede will follow the petition up with stories in his paper — and now you have no say over what he prints. My guess is that he'll follow the sheriff's tracks."

Pitman stood up and called for Jake Dill. When he appeared, Pitman said, "How many men can you get?"

"Ten to twenty," Dill said. "It depends on what you want them for."

Pitman ordered, "Just see that they're ready — all of them. I might decide that Gaptown isn't big enough for a newspaper."

"Better wait and see what's printed," Zinker suggested mildly.

"I'm waiting," Pitman shouted at him. "That's all I do — wait!"

Matt and Adam Bede reached town weary and cold in the saddle. Luther Colban, who was blacksmithing as if he had slept well all night, helped them from their horses.

"He holed up at Pitman's," Matt said.

"Wasted a night's ride," was Colban's brief answer. "The law is too weak, Matt."

"The law has to stay within the law," Matt retorted. "But at least we know the stories are true. Jake has joined with Pitman."

"Everyone knew it," Colban said.

"But now Matt has proof," Adam Bede said, without censure. "Let's go eat."

The breakfast rush, such as it was, had ended at Daisy's, and they had the place to themselves. She fixed pancakes and coffee, and watched them take the edge off their hunger before she spoke.

"Jud was in," she said. She glanced from Matt to Adam Bede.

"Adam's all right," Matt said. "He rides a straight trail, Daisy."

"Then," she said, "I'll tell it. Since you found Jud with that last beef he's stuck to mining. He follows my orders, Matt."

"I'm glad to hear it," Matt said.

"But yesterday," she went on, "his six-man train was moving ore down to the highway to be ready when the freight starts again. He says it was Dill's crew that hit him. He lost two men."

"And he wants to hit back," Matt said. He nodded his understanding. "But if he goes against them now he'll lose everything. Tell him to wait, Daisy."

"He can get more men," she said. She hesitated, then blurted out, "Whenever you're ready, Jud will help."

The warmth and coffee were relaxing to Matt. He could barely hold his eyes open.

197

But enough life remained in his mind for him to remember what had happened last night. He said, "Tell him to be sure of his men."

Rising, he led the way outside. Stumbling sleepily, he went into the jail office. Toby was there, his head on the desk. Matt roused him. "Come and get some sleep."

Toby lifted his head, blinking. "All quiet," he said. "All quiet except for laughing." His face twisted as if he wanted to cry. "The law is the best joke of the winter, Matt."

"Let's get some sleep," Matt repeated.

Toby walked beside him. Adam Bede left them, going to his newspaper office which he had fixed up with sleeping quarters. Toby said, "Did you get to Jake?"

"Cole Pitman was shielding him."

Toby said thinly, "They won't hold off forever, now that you know they're together. You got to do something, Matt. Winter's about over."

"Just about," Matt agreed.

Leaving Toby at the house, Matt automatically turned toward Gail's. He went in, said, "I came to tell you that I rode back like I said I would," and fell on her couch, asleep.

Chapter Twelve

Gail stood over the couch, looking down at Matt. She stood that way for some time. In response, his long face was gentle and without stubbornness. But she knew, remembering all of his words, that this was not true. Matt would have called them convictions, but the results were the same as far as she could see. In his stubbornness he had been nearly killed, and he had let his would-be murderers go free.

"Law!" she muttered fiercely. She clenched her hands tightly. Due process of law — a smug-sounding phrase. Relaxing her hands, she turned toward the kitchen. Let him sleep. And let him keep his beliefs. They were part of him, and she was accepting him as he was, not as she wished him to be. Underneath, she did not really know if she wished him to be different.

Dinnertime came and went, and Matt continued to sleep. Dusk was coming when, looking out of the window, Gail saw a horse and rider turn from Hill onto State, heading toward her. She watched idly and then with more interest when she saw that the rider was a girl. She was at the door when the knock came.

It was Lucy Morgan. She and Gail had

met during the time of Matt's convalescence, and there was no strangeness between them. Gail held the door wide.
"Come in."

Lucy stepped inside quickly. The flush on
her cheeks was deeper than the cold and
her ride could account for. When she saw
Matt, she said, "I'd hoped to find him here."

"He comes whenever he can," Gail said,
without embarrassment. "Take off your
wraps and get warm. I can fix some coffee."
She looked closely into Lucy's face as she
held out her hands for the girl's leather coat
and riding hat. "You're in trouble?"

Lucy nodded, her bright eyes misting.
"My brother," she said. "Dave, he ——"

"Sit down," Gail said gently, as she broke
off. "Rest until I get the coffee."

When Matt awoke, it was to find Lucy
watching him. He lay dull and dazed for a
moment and then sat up. Gail came in from
the kitchen to tell him that supper was
nearly ready. He lay back, shook his head to
clear away the sleep, and then struggled to
his feet. The signs of weariness and pain
were still deep on his face.

"What is it?" he asked of Lucy.

"Dave," she said. "It's about your — your
raid of last night."

Matt watched her closely; as he knew

Dave Morgan well, it took little time for him to guess what had happened. "He didn't like my way of doing it?"

Lucy nodded. "He went out to finish the job at Shackville."

Her words made him fully aware of the implications. "The job," he repeated. "My job?"

"Yes. Dave has lost more beef lately, and he thought ——"

"I know what he thought," Matt broke in, with sudden harshness. "He thought we hadn't the nerve to finish what we'd started."

"Or that you didn't have men enough," she said. She looked steadily at Matt, her eyes challenging. "And that your law isn't fast enough or good enough. It's true, Matt. Everyone in town knows it but you."

"Why did you come to me?" he asked wonderingly.

"Dave and five men rode out," she explained. "They haven't come back."

"Only one more than we were," Matt said. "It wasn't my law that bothered Dave. He wanted a chance at Cole Pitman, and he thought he'd take it by going through Bald Leggett and Jake Dill."

Gail stood in the doorway. "What do you intend to do, Matt?"

"Get Dave," he said, turning slowly toward her.

"And arrest him?"

"I'd arrest Cole if he attacked Dave," Matt said simply.

Lucy lowered her head. Gail turned about and went into the kitchen. Matt looked from the empty doorway to the girl in the chair. "The law ——"

"I don't care what you do," she cried. "I'm just afraid there won't be anyone to do it to, that's all. I want you to find Dave."

"Come and eat," Gail said abruptly, from the kitchen. "A man needs food, no matter what he intends to do."

Matt ate quickly, feeling the steady silence. He did not linger over coffee this time but got up, as soon as he had finished, and went out. He rode alone this time, using a rented deep-chested black from Luther Colban's stable. The snow was still coming down as he followed the highway north, but it was still a thin fine snow, and there was no more than a film over the ice underfoot.

The horse was cautious, and Matt, unsure of him, did not ride too fast, so it was heavy dark when he reached the crest above Shackville. Nothing seemed changed. The big building still stood, smoke spiraling in the air and spreading out as it felt the weight

202

of the snow pressing down on it. Lights were neither more nor less numerous than before. He began to wonder if Lucy had told him what she feared rather than what had actually taken place.

Shortly after he started down the grade, a flaring match drew him to the left. A cautious voice called, "Matt!"

Matt turned his horse into the brush. A man, mounted, sat there. He was smoking, and with each drag of his cigarette the hard dark planes of his face were lighted, showing his weariness. He let the light from the match glitter on the forty-four that he rested on the pommel of his saddle.

"Pat Ryan," he said, identifying himself as Morgan's foreman.

"Where's Dave?"

"I'm waiting for him," Ryan said. His voice was slow. "He went after a pair that hit into the hills."

"Then the fight is over?"

"The fight is over." Ryan's voice was dull with the weight of bitterness. "Two of the boys were downed, but they started for home. One is over yonder — he won't get up."

"And you?"

"All right," Ryan said. He added, "I was set here to stop you. Dave expected Lucy would ride in and that you'd be along."

"That's the way it worked out," Matt said.

"I'm to tell you that Bald Leggett still holds the aces," Pat Ryan said. "They lost no men, unless Dave finds the two that ran for the hills."

"Which way did Dave go?"

"West."

"That's Jud Keppel's territory," Matt said.

"Dave might be figuring on herding them to where Jud can find them," Pat Ryan remarked dryly.

Matt stirred in the saddle. "Ride home, Pat. When Dave comes in, bring him to town. You're all under arrest."

"I told Dave that would be the way of it," Ryan said, "but he figured to save you from going to Leggett's and getting shot anyway. A man has no chance to defend himself in this country any more."

"The law is here to do the defending."

Ryan led the way onto the road. They went side by side until a thin path went up the hills toward the north end of the Double M. Ryan nodded to Matt.

"If the law is here to do the defending, Matt, let it begin. Your law is worse than no law. So Dave said, and it's the truth. As for coming in and asking to be put in your jail, we don't intend to."

Matt watched as he put his horse up the sharp initial rise. Both looked for a moment as if they would go down, but finally the grade was made and they disappeared over the top.

Matt rode on for town, thinking over Pat Ryan's words. The law took time, he told himself. It always took time for men to accept new things. He did not doubt the correctness of the law, though he was beginning to doubt his own ability in enforcing it. Still he could not countenance open flouting of the law. And Dave Morgan's ride on Shackville, no matter what the outcome, was no more than a challenge to him.

Violence of this kind could only lead to more violence until the result was open warfare. And the quiet steady strength of law must be the restraining force. Any man could rule with enough guns — it was to fight that kind of rule that Matt had agitated for law in Gaptown.

Once his horse was back in the livery, he started his rounds. At Lamont's, where he went first, he met amused glances. Lamont came toward him. "I heard about Shackville," he said. "Maybe you'd better take your business out of here, Sheriff."

Matt looked around, but there was nothing out of the way, nothing out of the ordinary. He left, feeling men's smiles and laughter. He did not go to Hewitt's but returned to his office to sit silently until the town closed and he could return home to bed.

It was on Friday that he received word of Dave Morgan's return. Lucy had stayed with Gail, and now Matt went there to offer the girl a ride home. Gail spoke to him as she had done lately, drawn into herself, making no more conversation than necessary. He had refused her meals and her refuge since his last ride to Shackville; neither of them made a point of the subject.

"Dave is home," Matt said briefly.

Lucy thanked Gail, gathered her things, and went silently with Matt. It had been midmorning when they left, and dinner was just over when they reached the cluster of ranch buildings. Dave Morgan walked onto the veranda and invited Matt in. "Thanks for bringing Lucy," he said.

"I have business here," Matt answered. He did not like this, and yet he could see no other way of making the law felt except to enforce it.

"Pat told me," Dave said. "I missed Dill's two men, by the way." He sat down, looking comfortable. "But we found them yesterday, hanging to a low-branched pine. I'm satisfied."

"I'm not," Matt said. "I'll wait while you and the boys get ready, Dave."

Old Pete Morgan came out of the other room, wheeling rapidly in his chair, a forty-four in his lap. He looked coldly at Matt. "Don't bring your law up here, Matt. Not while Pitman and Dill and Leggett go free to laugh."

"Be quiet," Dave said. "I'll go with Matt. Pat and the three boys are ready. Two weren't hit bad. The one still in the brush is beyond the law." He smiled at Matt, smiled and waited.

His father said irately, "Five of you gone. Are you crazy to leave the place to me and a couple of wranglers?"

"That's Matt's law," Dave Morgan said, in the same quiet tone. "After Pitman finds we're in jail and comes and takes our place, then Matt can arrest him, too. The law does the defending; Matt said so himself."

Matt looked from one to the other, from the ominously placid son to the angry old man whose finger was trembling on the trigger of his gun. But it was not that which decided him. Nor was it the loss of the Morgan friendship. It was the bitter realization that his months of working to establish law were as nothing. Because Dave Morgan was right. Let him take his strength from here, and Pitman would be down, vulturelike. And all of the arresting of Pitman later would mean nothing. It would not bring back the lives lost nor the buildings burned. The law would be more than a laughing stock, it would be an instrument of destruction.

Matt turned to go. Lucy Morgan stepped up to him and touched his arm. Great relief and great pity showed in her eyes. "It's as Gail says, Matt, this country isn't ready yet for your kind of law."

"So I know," he said, and went out.

In town he walked to Abe Parkis' office and repeated those things. "I can't stand for the law and act against it," Matt told Abe. "If the country isn't ready for law, one man like myself can't make it so. I'll not have the blood of my neighbors on my head." He put up a hand to take off his badge.

"They were right," Abe said. "You're too young."

"Perhaps," Matt said. "Or maybe I lack the courage of my convictions."

"No," Abe said. "You have too much conviction — and too much courage." He drew Matt's hand away from the badge. "Hold up a minute, Matt, and listen to me."

Out of respect for Abe, and because the shock of his utter defeat had taken some of the spirit from him, Matt lowered his hand. "I'm waiting," he said.

"Sometimes," Abe began, "what a man calls courage is plain bullheadedness. You're sure that your way is right, and you want to prove it — all by yourself. Did you ever stop to think that there are others in this town who want to see law and order, too? Others that have a big stake in things? Maybe they'd like to help."

"Like Luther," Matt said. " 'Burn them out.' "

"Ah," Abe said. "Your way of going at it hasn't worked. Maybe their way will. Law by force can be the right kind of law, Matt, if it's controlled force. And it has to be that kind of law — now. You can't fight a forty-four with a muzzle-loading popgun. Not until you draw the bite out of the forty-four."

Matt stood with his hands at his sides. He said after a moment, "Call Adam in, Abe, and Luther and the rest."

When they had come, including Ira Morris and Lippy Hollister, Matt said, "If you want law by force, I can give you law by force. But it means that every man of you will have to fight — not just me. It means

209

slapping Cole Pitman in the teeth — and he won't stand by and take it. If you agree, I'll deputize every man of you. And you'll be deputies until Cole is done or we're burned out.

"It's your choice."

There was no hesitation, no questioning. Without waiting, Matt went through the formality of swearing them in as deputies. Then, taking his hat, he started for the door.

"Just remember," he said, "to keep your women and children off the streets after dark." He walked out.

Saturday night was clear and cold. The last strength of winter sent sharp icy air pouring down into the gap, so that men and horses came into town stamping and blowing. It took more whiskey to thaw a man out than it had taken to make him drunk in the summer.

And from the sounds, Matt thought, every man within a day's ride of Gaptown had come in to do the thawing. He lay on a bunk at the rear of Adam Bede's shop next door to Abe Parkis'. Matt's forty-four was handy, and a Sharps rifle lay by the bunk. Adam Bede's first paper had come out the day before, and Matt knew that the newspaperman would need protection.

For that reason, he had decided on a course of strategy: instead of taking the law to men, he was going to let the men come to the law.

"To go by myself into the saloons would be no different from before," he told Adam. "Let them think we're even weaker. If this is war, then I'll use the tactics of war — force and strategy."

At eleven that night, with the noise of the saloons flowing over the town as it had not done since before Matt took the badge, Adam went out and brought back sandwiches and coffee.

"All quiet," he said. "Lots of drinking, but not much else."

"Maybe I'm wrong," Matt admitted. "Maybe there was nothing in your paper to make anyone angry."

"It depends on how you read the paper," Adam answered. "There were implications in my story on Shackville that Cole Pitman won't favor. Nor will Ezra Meecham appreciate my editorial questioning his right to oust our one and only schoolteacher." His face screwed into a wry grin beneath his beard. "But Ezra should be happy, Matt. Listen to the gold pouring into the saloon tills!"

Matt went to the door and peered down

the street. Then he returned to the bunk. "That's more noise than just another test of the weakness of the law would bring, Adam. You may be right about Pitman. It looks to me as if every rough within forty miles has been ordered into Gaptown."

Bede said soberly, "Pitman is a man who wants everything, including the respect of the community. The things I've printed are nothing to the things I can print. He knows this, and he may try to destroy me because of it."

"So I'm guessing," Matt agreed. "Or I wouldn't be here." He turned to his sandwich and coffee. Adam Bede announced that he was going to look around and went away.

Matt ate and then lay on the cot. He was thinking of Toby. He had not taken the boy into consideration when he had started his new plan and Toby, realizing that to stay with Matt now would mean fighting his own father sooner or later, had resigned. Now Matt wondered if Toby would return to the mine and his old ways. It was a souring thought.

At midnight someone knocked on the door. It was Toby Dill. Matt let him in. Toby stood before him; panting and reeking a little of whiskey.

"I've been dancing at Lamont's and drinking at Hewitt's," he said.

"What is that to me?" Matt asked him.

Toby stood straight; he sounded fully sober. "Some of Jake's crew were around." His face was a blur in the darkness. "A dance-hall girl I know told me. They're coming, Matt, to burn this place out. That's why everybody is in town — to help burn it. Jake brought them in on Cole's orders."

"So I figured," Matt said. "But why are you telling me this — on Jake?"

"Not on Jake, on his crew," Toby answered. "You gave me a break, Matt, and no one else has ever done that. You even understood why I had to quit being deputy, and you didn't get sore about it. I'll try to head Jake off. But you get out. Even if they don't know you're here and you can surprise 'em, you can't fight twenty or thirty."

"Every man except Ezra on this end of Main Street is deputized," Matt said. "And a couple from the south end. I don't lack strength. Go tell Adam for me, Toby, then ride clear. Warn Jake if you want, but keep yourself out of it."

Toby sounded as if he might cry. "You ride yourself, Matt. You can't fight Jake's men. They're primed with whiskey. And there ain't time to round up anybody. There ain't much time left at all."

"Get going," Matt ordered sharply. He watched Toby go at a stumbling run, then he returned to the cot, checked his guns, and sat to wait for Adam.

When he came, he said, "Toby found me. I didn't have time to get to Abe and the others. I think Jake's crew is on its way now." He sounded as calm as if he were dealing an easy game in the saloon.

Matt said, "We'll get on the roof and try to keep them far enough off so they can't start a fire."

"But we need more men," Adam said, looking to his gun. "Maybe if I made a break for ——"

"Not now," Matt interrupted. "The saloons are too quiet. There isn't any time — Toby was right."

They ran into the alley and up to the roof by a rickety wall ladder. It was a flattish roof, with just enough pitch for drainage, and had a low parapet surrounding it. Matt squatted on his heels, looking over the edge, keeping himself in line with the chimney so that his silhouette wouldn't show against the starlight of the sky. Adam crouched low beside him.

"They'll come from State," Matt guessed. "They're probably getting together behind

Hewitt's, ready to ride into the alley here." His voice was pitched low.

"Let them come," Adam Bede said. "They don't think there's law enough to stop them now."

They were still, listening. The sound of many hoofs, ringing sharply on the frozen ground, came up to them suddenly. Adam eased himself forward a little. Matt did not move.

"They're coming from both ways down the alley, Adam," he said.

CHAPTER THIRTEEN

Gail sat by her parlor window, mending by lamplight until her eyes and fingers refused to work together any longer. Then she blew out the light and looked at the darkness of State Street. From this window she had a glimpse of one corner of Matt's house and, in the opposite direction, a corner of the boardinghouse. Between the two was open ground reaching to the alley, and she had a clear view of the rear of Adam's shop. She watched it now because Adam had told her Matt would be there.

I helped force him into it, she thought. She knew that he had not taken this new step because of her, and yet she could not keep from shouldering part of the blame, woman fashion. He had sworn himself to force, and he had not returned to her since. That lay heavily in her mind, and she rocked in her chair as though to rid herself of the ideas by the violence of her motion.

"I'm a fool," she said aloud. She could go to the rear of the shop and call to him, she thought. But she had pride, the same kind of pride that had driven her cousin Ellen to her death. And Matt was no man to crawl to. She would go to him if he called, yes. But she would go straight, her head up.

Rising, she replenished the fire and, as an afterthought, put water on to heat. Perhaps after his work was done he would come for coffee and talk. She smiled thinly at her own wishful thinking and returned to her seat. She looked again at the rear of the shop; she could see quite plainly, as there was no light in the room to reflect on the window-pane.

How long she sat she did not know. Perhaps she dozed. She was not aware of her thoughts until she saw the men coming up State, over a dozen of them, riding softly. They came across Hill, passed her house, and at the end of the street turned west toward the alley. She watched them idly. Riders were no great curiosity even along

State Street. But suddenly she realized that they were too silent for the average group of drunken roisterers. Too silent and too cautious in their movements.

When she saw the direction in which they were heading, she rose quickly. The reason Adam needed protection was plain enough to her. His newspaper lay on the table within easy reach of her hand, and she knew Cole Pitman well enough to realize what his reaction would be to the veiled hints contained in the story on Shackville.

Getting a shawl for her head, she ran out of the house just as the horsemen spurred from either direction toward the rear of the shop. She could see clearly now and she ran, half stumbling over the rough frozen ground, toward Abe Parkis' house a short distance away. Though she had never been asked to call there, she did not hesitate. Running to the porch, she jerked the bell pull. A ringing came from inside. She kept pulling, frantically, until her arm felt as if it would drop from her shoulder. Finally she heard a bolt being thrown back.

It was Abe, carrying a lamp and wearing his nightshirt. She opened her mouth to speak and the first sharp hard shots cracked on the icy air.

Abe said, "In here, quick," and shut the

217

door behind her.

"They're attacking — at Adam's."

He thrust the lamp at her and raced into another room. When he came back he had a greatcoat, pants, and boots on. He carried an old Henry rifle, and he went out hurriedly, not speaking to her.

Gail sat, emptily. The sounds of shooting ceased for a moment and then rose to a crescendo of sound from which she could pick out no single shot. A horse screamed shrilly, making her shiver. With a sudden gasp, she rose and fled from the house. At her own place, she got the thirty-eight Matt had let her keep, pushed a box of ammunition into her dress pocket, and ran across State toward the alley.

Matt held his fire until both groups of men had converged less than ten feet apart beneath him. His was the first shot, and a man threw up his hands and crashed out of the saddle onto the hard ground.

"Amazing," Bede murmured. He fired his rifle. Matt followed with three quick bursts from his forty-four. The men in the alley spread, one of them cursing viciously, another moaning from where he lay under the hoofs of the milling horses.

Matt reloaded as he waited. He was suddenly aware that he felt no compunction at all. This was violence and, technically, he had begun it. The men below had made no move but to ride up, had given no indication that they would attack. He had to admit to himself that he had only Toby's word that they would attack. He had begun this by violence and he saw that it could end only by violence. Coldly, deliberately, he set the Sharps and waited.

The answer came as soon as the surprised men below had had time to fade to more advantageous positions in the shadows below. A concerted burst of fire raked the roof, tipping splinters from the parapet, tearing pieces of brick from the chimney. There was no answer from the roof, and the fire became spasmodic. Matt continued his silence until his sights were well lined on a patch of black that was too dark for shadow. When a spurt of flame came from the patch, he squeezed the trigger. A man's cry of pain rose on the night and then burbled out. From two sides answering fire searched out Matt, and a splinter of wood lanced his cheek, sending warm blood down his chin and neck. Adam was shooting coolly beside him, and after another volley from below Matt reached out and dragged Adam down, halting his fire.

"Let them form again," he said.

They did as he expected, coming out of the shadows, firing as they rode, ripping the parapet up with their lead, forming in a loose group. A torch flared up.

"Now," Matt said, and he rose with his forty-four in his hand. Adam followed suit, and they sent a swift withering fire down onto the men below. A horse vented a shrill scream, two men plunged down, and the remaining riders broke, trying to force their way out as they had come.

"Our advantage up here," Bede murmured.

The torch someone carried down below flipped into the air as a deliberate shot sent its owner spinning.

"Nice shooting," Adam Bede said.

"Not from me," Matt said.

He understood as sharp firing came from both ends of the alley. The riders who were racing that way turned and came back, meeting each other in headlong flight and milling, unable to find their way about.

A voice called, begging for surrender. From the thin light of the stars Matt could make out hands raised in the air, and then silence fell. Lights began to appear, from men carrying lanterns and from windows lighted at the rear of the boardinghouse.

220

Matt and Adam came down the ladder.

There were still eight men mounted. Two stood horseless, their hands raised, and a dozen were on the ground, though only one seemed past repairing.

"Two must have escaped," Bede remarked cheerfully. "I calculated an even dozen."

Abe Parkis pushed his way forward, his coat open to show his nightshirt, his old Henry rifle in his hands. Matt stepped out to meet him. "Go easy with the wounded," Matt ordered. "Haul that dead one away. The rest of you get to jail."

Cole Pitman worked himself through the crowd that had formed in the mouth of the alley. "You letting Abe here get away carrying a gun, Sheriff?"

Abe Parkis shifted his rifle. "I'm a legal deputy, Pitman," he said, in his rusty voice.

Amusement in Matt, brought on by the look of consternation on Pitman's face, fought with uneasiness at all this, the result of the violence he had begun. He said sharply, "Clear the alley."

Toby came up. "Jake and a pair hit for the hills," he said, in a low voice. "Jake went first." He looked up at Matt. "I got him with my gun butt. He knows it was me, but I couldn't stand by and see him shot up. I better drift, Matt."

221

"Jake will be in jail soon enough," Matt said.

"Jake ain't easy to hold onto," Toby said quietly. Turning, he slipped down the alley into darkness.

Slowly the crowd dispersed. With Abe's help and the help of a few other of his deputies, Matt herded Dill's crew into jail. Abe came back from closing a cell; he was chuckling.

"They say you started it, Matt."

"So I did," Matt admitted.

"We were defending property," Adam Bede said.

Matt said, "Are you two enjoying trying to rile me? It's enough that Jake Dill got away." To take the sting off his words, he added, "Thanks for the help, Abe. You and the others."

" 'The others' was that Winter girl," Abe answered. "She was standing spang in the open, emptying a horse pistol at them." He paused, spitting. "You going after Dill?"

"Soon," Matt said.

Abe looked thoughtful at the bitter note in Matt's voice. But he only said, "The girl went home, Matt."

Matt could see a light in Gail's window, and he hurried across State and up to her porch.

She had the door open before he could knock.

"I came to thank you," he said awkwardly.

The lamplight touched him, and she saw blood on his face. "You're hurt." Taking his hands, she drew him inside and closed the door.

"I can't stay," he protested.

"Adam will know where you are," she said. "And he doesn't need you now, anyway. I have some hot water, some coffee —" She turned away, getting the water and a cloth. The splinter lay half embedded in his cheek. Without hesitation, she reached up and pulled it out, staunching the fresh flow of blood with a quick movement of the cloth.

"You're all right now," she said, after a moment. "Coffee?"

"I'm welcome again?" he asked.

"I never denied you welcome," she answered. Turning aside, she came back with the coffee. "What would have happened tonight if you had — had followed your former ideas?"

"There wouldn't have been any killing," Matt answered stubbornly. "I would have tried to round them up before they could form for an attack."

"Another Shackville," she said quietly.

223

"And Adam's press would be scrap by now. Do you believe you could have stopped them, Matt?"

He lowered his eyes to his coffee, blowing on the surface with exaggerated care. "I don't know," he admitted. He moved restlessly. "I do know that it won't stop here. The law threw out a challenge tonight. There'll be retaliation."

"By Pitman?"

He nodded. "What Dill's men tried to do tonight was done on Pitman's order. I felt it would happen. That's why I went to Adam's as I did."

She drew a deep breath. "I thought as much. It's one more thing. One more thing on top of all the others Cole has done." She shook her head slowly. "But you can't fight him, Matt. He's too strong. You can't fight him, not even with his own weapons."

"I plan to draw him out," Matt said. "Weaken him little by little. Drawn out, maybe he can be picked off at the edges."

"You — alone?"

"So I intended," Matt said. "Tonight Abe and the others came to help. Now Cole knows — if he didn't know before — that we're banded together. He won't stop at attacking just Adam and me. He'll go after them, too — any way he can." He paused and sipped his coffee. "By going alone, I hoped to keep them out of it as long as possible."

"You get help even when you don't want it," she said. "They don't want to be kept out of it. Neither do I."

He looked at her, not understanding. She smiled thinly and picked up her shawl. "Come with me," she ordered.

"What are you going to do?"

"A woman should always help her man," Gail answered, and led him outside.

As they approached Bede's shop, Matt began to understand her intention and the meaning of her words. He caught her by the arm. "Wait," he said. "People will talk — about you."

"They couldn't say any more than they have said." She opened the door to the shop and walked in.

Adam Bede was prowling around his press, sniffing the ink smells and looking fondly at the ungainly mass of iron that had come so laboriously from the coast.

"Adam," Gail said quietly. He turned. She went on, her voice steady. "I have a story for your paper." Adam Bede came up to her, his eyebrows lifted in silent questioning.

"It's about Cole Pitman," she said. "Cole and a girl."

■ ■ ■ ■

It was worth an extra edition, Bede decided. And with the suppressed excitement characteristic of him, he put both Matt and Gail to work. By sunrise on Sunday morning, a one-sheet edition of his paper was ready for distribution.

Matt picked the first sheet out of the press, his fingers smearing the damp ink across the page. It was six columns with EXTRA in large type across the top. Below was a fine design that Adam had created for himself: the Territorial and Federal flags, their staffs crossed and joined by an eagle. Underneath that was *Gaptown Gazette* in fancy lettering. Matt ran his eyes down the columns. The first was headed, PERFIDY OF LOCAL CITIZEN. Matt noted with grim amusement that though Cole Pitman's name was blazoned in every paragraph there was nothing said that could be interpreted as other than factual. The opposite column had the headline, SHERIFF DEPUTIZES LOCAL CITIZENRY. Matt looked at Adam Bede, who seemed too busy to return the glance. Matt read the article, which not only mentioned his recent action but gave a detailed account of the night's attack. In

226

some way, Bede had managed to get Pitman's name into this article as well.

"Adam," Matt said when he had finished reading, "you've succeeded in making Cole the cause of everything but the weather."

Bede chuckled. "Wait and see," he said happily. "Wait and see."

By nightfall, Matt was slumped wearily in his own parlor. Toby and Adam Bede were there, both watching the dark street from the front window. Although Toby had not taken up Matt's offer to be deputy again, he had agreed not to ride on — not just yet. For the boy's sake, Matt insisted he continue to live with him.

They were all weary, having got only a little sleep during the day. Most of the time had been spent seeing a steady stream of readers, all of whom wanted to know more details on the story Adam's extra had carried. The answer was the same to all: they had to wait until the regular Friday edition.

Bede was exultant. "I told you, Matt. Over half the town is ready to spit on Cole Pitman. He's a leper. Ah, the power of words!"

"Pitman will make you swallow a few," Toby prophesied darkly. "Wait until he gets a look at the paper."

"Bring him into the open," Bede said. "It's

time for a showdown."

Matt wished it were all as simple as Bede seemed to think. Those people who were ready to spit on Pitman, as Bede put it, could change back as fast as they had swung away from him. A ready explanation, a cocky attitude — either or both would turn a lot of opinions. Matt only hoped that Pitman, in his impatience, wouldn't wait to attempt an explanation.

"I agree that it's time for a showdown," Matt said. "But I dislike being sheriff while it's happening." He looked down at his big hands, started to speak again. "I ——"

"Riders coming," Toby interrupted harshly.

"Ah," Bede murmured. "Now we'll see." He leaned forward, peering into the darkness. "It can't be anyone else but Pitman."

They sat silently, waiting. The only movement was that of Matt checking his gun load. Toby said, "Three men is all," and faded from the window.

When the knock came, Matt went to the door and opened it. Cole Pitman stood there. "I hear Bede is here," he said. "I want him."

"A man's home is his castle," Matt said, mocking him. "There must be a refuge somewhere."

Adam Bede walked into Pitman's view. "Good evening," he said pleasantly. "You'll be glad to know that I can pay off your note soon. My papers sell extremely well."

"Damn your paper!" Pitman cried. "I want a retraction on the lies you've printed."

"Lies?" Bede's voice was softly querying.

Cole Pitman inserted himself a step into the room. "The impression you gave ——"

From the darkness outside, a voice said, "Patience, Captain."

Adam Bede kept his smile. "Let's see, how is this for the next headline: 'Pitman Preys on Printer. Leading Rancher Reads Between the Lines.' "

"By God!" Pitman burst out. He made a move for his gun, but Matt's hand clamped over his wrist.

"Not here, not ever," he warned softly.

Pitman stood motionless, staring into Matt's impassive face. His eyes were squeezed half shut with anger. It burst out through his lips, unable to be controlled any longer.

"There won't be another edition of the paper, Bede." He swung on his boot heel and strode down the steps.

Matt stood where he was until he heard the creak of saddle leather. Then he shut the door. Adam Bede was smiling, but Toby had a scowl on his face.

"He ain't through," Toby said. "He's crazy mad right now. Zinker won't keep him quiet much longer. He'll take it out on anyone he can. Anything he can. The shop ——"

Matt came alive. "The shop be damned," he cried. "Gail is over there, alone. And it was her story that started this."

Jerking open the door, he ran into the cold icy night. He raced across State, through a yard, and down the alley behind the houses that faced westward. There was a light in Gail's and, tied by the rear door, a single horse. Without waiting, Matt went into the kitchen and drew up in the doorway of the living room.

He was right. This was Pitman's way of doing things, his pattern of living. He was fighting the world by charging in, bulling his way through. Matt heard his angry, hot words.

"You'll pack and go — tonight. I'll furnish the horse and have you escorted south. When the stage comes to the Falls, you'll be on it. That's all."

Matt said from the doorway, "You drove one woman to her death. Let that be enough."

Pitman was in the center of the room, and Gail stood near the far wall. When she saw

Matt the rigidity went from her shoulders, and she pressed herself to the wall for support. Pitman turned, making a move for his gun.

But Matt was faster, his advantage being that of surprise. "Now," he said, his gun out, "we'll see about your order. Gail, take his gun."

She did so, and Matt removed his coat, tossing it and his gun to the sofa. She went there and sat, holding both guns loosely at her sides.

"You're a man of force," Matt said. "I'll give you force."

Pitman measured Matt's rawboned looseness against his own compact bulk and smiled. "I've seen your force before — Sheriff."

CHAPTER FOURTEEN

Matt advanced toward Pitman, the lamplight showing up the hard set planes of his face. Pitman waited with what seemed amused insolence. If he thought of Gail there with the two guns, he gave no sign.

Matt made his first rush suddenly. Pitman laughed softly and stepped aside, his fist catching Matt on the mouth. The rush carried Matt forward and onto one knee. He turned, raising his shoulder as Pitman lashed out with a foot.

Matt came to his feet and rushed again. His shoulder felt numb from the force of Pitman's kick. He held his head low and, when Pitman swung his fist again, threw himself sideways, hitting Pitman at the knees and sending him against an armchair. Matt fell on top and caught Pitman's arm. Rolling, he threw Pitman over his head. Pitman landed with his back flat to the floor, the breath crashing hard from between his lips.

When Matt reached him, Pitman was on one knee. He got to his feet in time to meet Matt's fist, ducking to one side to ease the force of the blow. He lashed out with both arms, hammering at Matt's heart, making Matt give ground. Matt came forward again doggedly, blocking a blow with his sore shoulder and closing in to get a bear hug.

Pitman hammered him in the ribs while Matt hung tenaciously, trying to throw him from his feet. But he could get no leverage and he let go, taking a fist in the eye. His swinging hand caught Pitman on the nose, bringing a spurt of blood. Pitman backed off, more wary now. The grogginess caused by his fall seemed to have passed, and when Matt rushed he stepped easily aside.

Matt could not get in close after that. Pitman's fists became dull knives that ripped at his face and heart. The wind was going from him and the sap was running out as fast as the blood from the cuts on his face. When he shook his head to clear it, Pitman took the advantage and stepped in close.

Matt fell against him in a tight clinch and let Pitman hammer on his ribs while he worked to get breath. Then, without warning, he swung as if he were dancing a waltz. Pitman's feet lost their stance, and Matt threw him in the opposite direction without letting loose his grip. They crashed to the floor, smashing a chair as they went down, turning its remains over on top of them.

Pitman was the first man to his feet. Except for the blood on his nose, he seemed as fresh and untouched as he had been at the beginning. He stood, his knees bent, waiting for Matt to reach his feet. Matt lay a moment, sucking air, and then pushed himself up. The walls weaved in at him. His lips were puffed and his nose so filled with blood that it was hard to breathe.

Gail had moved from the couch to the doorway. She emptied both guns of bullets and put everything on a kitchen chair. She resumed her watching, her face impassive. She could stop it, she knew, simply by clubbing Pitman with a gun butt. But this was not her way, nor was it the way Matt would want.

Matt saw Pitman come forward, swinging, but he could not dodge the blow. Instead, when it landed, he fell forward and slightly to one side. The fist raked his cheek and spun him into Pitman. He did not try to clinch now but leaned against Pitman's chest. The dizziness left him even though Pitman was striking his heart with steady driving blows. With an effort, Matt drew back his arm, stepped to one side, and lashed out with all the weight of his body. His anger, his frustration, his bitterness at the things Pitman represented went into what he knew to be his last possible effort.

His fist caught Pitman under the breastbone, where he had not expected it. Matt felt the iron-hardness of the man yield to the crushing force, and then his own strength was gone and he stumbled back. He heard Pitman retch, gasping for the air that would not come.

Pitman made feeble motions with his hands, as if to drag the air back into himself. Matt staggered forward and hit him weakly in the face with his head. He could not do much damage, but when Pitman toppled he fell on top. They lay a moment, neither man able to move; then Matt found the strength to lift his fists, and he began drumming Pitman's face.

His strength grew briefly, and his fists flailed more strongly. Then his knuckles slipped on the blood that was flowing and he desisted, rolling away and getting groggily to his feet. He looked down at Pitman and then fell himself, stretching alongside the unconscious man. A faint cloud of dust rose from the rug and settled about them both.

Gail moved, getting water and pouring it on Matt until he came to. After a moment he rose to his feet and staggered to the couch. When he could, he stood again and went back to Pitman.

"Matt!"

He looked at her through eyes almost swollen shut. "This is law by force, Gail."

Without further words, he bent and caught Pitman by the collar. Slowly, painfully, he dragged the heavier man outside and onto the porch. It took some time, as he needed frequent periods of rest, but at last he had Pitman belly down across his own saddle. Then, taking the reins of the horse, Matt walked stolidly down State to Hill, to Main, and southward to Lamont's saloon. He tied the horse carefully to the hitch rack, jerked

Pitman out of the saddle, and, with the same slow movements, dragged the man across the boardwalk and through the batwing doors.

Texas Zinker and Pitman's men were at the bar, waiting as they had been told to do. When Matt came slowly into the room, the noise of dancing and talk faded and died. The clink of chips and the rustle of cards slid off into silence, and for a moment there was nothing but the sounds of men's breathing.

Deliberately, Matt drew Cole Pitman to the center of the dance floor and turned him loose. Pitman's head thudded to the polished boards, and he lay as he had at Gail's — inert, his mouth open, blood slowly drying on his battered face.

Matt looked at Zinker and at Pitman's men. "Take him home and keep him there," he said.

Someone stirred at the bar. Zinker raised a hand, his voice calm. "No," he said. "This is the sheriff's round."

"I'm the law," Matt said quietly. He focused his eyes on Zinker with an obvious effort. "Tell Jake Dill I'm coming after him — as myself, and as the law."

He walked out, slowly retracing his steps to Gail's house. Inside, he carefully laid himself on the sofa. His eyes closed and his head fell back. Gail went for more warm water. She thought without humor that she would have done better to have learned nursing when she went to school.

Matt's beating was superficial, and within a few days he was up and about. Saying nothing even to Gail, he loaded his saddlebags with food, mounted his sorrel, and rode from town. He left at daybreak, and by full dark he was back. He fell into his bunk, once his horse was seen to, and slept until early the next morning. Rising, he washed up and went to Daisy's for his breakfast.

She was just opening, and the smell of coffee was fresh in the air. Matt sat at the counter, drinking a cupful while she fried him some hotcakes.

"Jud was in late yesterday," Daisy said. "Jake and some of the Shackville crew raided him again last night." Matt made no answer, and she went on, "He didn't have men enough, and it was only that little canyon of his that saved him."

"Why tell me?" Matt demanded.

"Jud figured you'd go on to Shackville to finish what you started with Pitman," Daisy answered. "He's offering his help."

"I'll need it," Matt agreed. "I rode to

Jake's mine, but it's abandoned. He can't be anywhere else but Shackville. Or Pitman's."

"He's at Shackville," Daisy said. "Jud knows that much."

Matt took a deep gulp of the hot coffee. "Tell Jud to meet me at the first bend north of town — at sundown."

"Ah," Daisy said, pleased. "I'm glad to hear that, Matt."

Matt slept during the day, first dropping a word about his plans to Adam Bede as well as to Daisy. He wasn't surprised to see a crew of men waiting for him when he reached the first north bend in the freight highway. He counted twenty-two, including Jud Keppel and seven he had brought with him.

Matt said dryly, "Those of you who aren't already deputies — step forward." They did so, and Matt deputized them quickly. No one spoke; no one smiled at this.

Matt said, "We'll send a warning." His voice was flat. "Any innocent man can get out. After that we burn them."

"Good enough," Luther Colban agreed.

Adam Bede rode alongside Matt. "What about Cole? He can have heard of this."

"Is he able to fight?" Matt asked, and led

the way down the road toward Shackville.

When they reached the crest above the prairie, Matt halted the men. Lights cast a pattern on dirty snow; smoke spiraled from the chimney of the big building and from the smaller chimneys of the cabins.

"We'll surround them and give warning," Matt said.

He led the way down, halting a good fifty yards from the main building. The men spread out, ringing the saloon and the shacks. The sound of hoofbeats on the frozen ground under the thin snow blanket were audible in the still night, yet no one appeared. No one made a move from any building. There was no sign that anything out of the ordinary was taking place.

Matt said to Adam Bede, "Something is wrong."

"They had time to be warned," Bede said. "It could be a trap."

"We'll go ahead," Matt decided. Without waiting for the others, he rode to the saloon door. His voice rose in warning. "Come out, Leggett. Every man out."

There was no sound. The lamplight came from inside and glittered on the cold snow. Smoke continued to rise in a slow straight column.

"Come out or be burned out!"

The silence oppressed him. He patted his sorrel and sat a moment, motionless in the saddle. Slowly the feeling came over him that this was some monstrous joke played by the night and the cold. Dropping to the ground, he walked to the door. It gave under his push and he went inside, gun in hand.

The room was empty. Blankness stared at him from the bar and from the tables. Dirty glasses were scattered about, but there was no one in sight. Matt took a deep unbelieving breath and started for the door. As if his movement was a signal, rapid gunfire crackled sharply on the air. Matt raced for the door; from the sound he knew that his men were being attacked.

The firing came from the small shacks and from the fringe of trees lining the road. Matt saw two men drop from their saddles and others spur wildly into the night. A few guns opened up from the posse, but there was no target to shoot at except the gunfire blossoming from the dark of the trees, and these were constantly shifting.

Matt heard a bullet suck air by his head as he leaped into the saddle. Spurring wildly, he bent low and raced out of the line of fire to where a group of his men were congregated.

"Trapped," Abe Parkis said bitterly.

Jud Keppel came riding into the group. "Two hurt," he said. "We got to ride or they'll ring us and cut off the road."

"We'll ride," Matt agreed. "Jud, take some men and try to clean out those cabins. Abe, you move a bunch south to the crest and work back north. I'll come south to meet you. We have to flush them from the trees."

"We'll flush ourselves into graves," was Abe Parkis' comment.

"Then ride home — if you can get there." Matt reined around. "Adam?"

"We might as well shoot them," Bede answered, with bitter humor. "They don't buy my papers anyway."

Six men went with Matt. There was no firing as they worked their way upslope. Shackville was as silent as when they had come. At the top of the first rise, Matt reined into the brush. There were no trails plain enough to be seen; it was a matter of giving the horses their heads. Shortly, Matt said, "Far enough. Stake the horses."

Leaving one man to watch their mounts, they went forward on foot, striving for caution. But branches that were barely snow-covered cracked beneath their weight, and bushes rustled loudly as they blundered against them in the thick darkness.

"We need light," Matt said, in a low tone.

Adam Bede put a hand out, touching Matt's arm. A moment later he could be heard bulling through the brush toward the road. Ahead of them the silence still held.

From the direction of the buildings the sounds of gunfire came suddenly. Jud Keppel was making an attack, Matt thought. "Move on," he ordered.

They made slow progress, stopping every half-dozen paces to listen. Matt strained his eyes in the forest blackness, but he could scarcely make out the bole of a tree, let alone a waiting man. Eternity crept by, and then a roaring came from Shackville on their left. Light blossomed into the sky, flailing against the night, and a rich crackling sound drowned out all other noise. The light pushed through the fringe of forest, throwing shadow patterns and highlighting the startled faces of the men.

"Adam done that!" Luther Colban said, from behind Matt. "That fire won't leave a cockroach alive. I can feel the heat back here."

"Spread out," Matt ordered sharply. "They have as much light as we have."

They separated hurriedly. The light grew as Shackville's big wooden saloon burned more fiercely. Matt made out a vague form in front of him, a man crouched with a rifle in his hands. Obviously he had been waiting for the posse to come close enough to be ambushed again, and the fire had caught him by surprise. Matt flipped up his forty-four and fired. The man eased back into the snow-covered brush and out of sight.

As if the shot were a signal, guns broke out ahead. Behind Matt, a man cried out wildly and flung himself into the bushes. The volley ceased as quickly as it had begun, and everything was silent again but for the now steady crackling of the fire.

Working around a tree, Matt came on another Shackville man. He missed with his first shot and fired again. But now the man was running and dodging, firing back as he ran. His gun emptied suddenly, and he flung it at Matt, who was racing after him. Matt holstered his own forty-four and followed over a rise in the ground to a small cleared space. The other tripped over a half-exposed root, and Matt pinned him to the ground with a long driving leap. The man wriggled and slashed with bare hands, and Matt drove a knee down cruelly. The man grunted and went limp.

Matt dragged him out of shadow. He recognized one of Dill's men. Pulling the man's belt free, Matt roped his hands behind his back. Deliberately he took out his gun. "Now," he said. "How many here?"

"Go to hell, Ross."

Matt cut the sight of the gun across the man's cheek, making a shallow furrow that oozed blood slowly. "How many?"

"Four here. Four across the road. Six in the cabins."

"Where's Dill?"

The man shook his head. Matt raked him again with the gun sight, crossing the first wound to form an X. The man said, whimpering, "In one of the cabins."

Luther Colban eased up. Matt said, "How many did you get?"

"Three back there. They got Ira Morris in the leg."

"That's all, then," Matt said. "Unless this one is lying."

"I ain't," the man cried.

Luther Colban studied the gun in Matt's hand and then the man's bleeding face. "Getting rough, ain't you, Matt?"

"Law by force," Matt said. He added, "Watch this one," and faded toward the road. Once there his eyes were dazzled by the brightness of the huge flaming building. He crossed the road where a tongue of forest came out on the other side and worked his way cautiously toward the clearing.

When he was on the inside edge of the fringe of timber he could see Abe Parkis leading a charge, Indian-fashion, around the shacks, and he relaxed his caution. Abe obviously had cleaned out the four on his side of the road.

One shack was aflame, and Abe's riders were trying to set a blaze in the other, but a careful fire from the two windows drove them back each time they swung in close with their lighted torches. All at once the door of the fired shack burst open and a man came running from it. Matt recognized the lumbering gait of Bald Leggett. Without hesitation, Matt dashed forward, into the open. But he was not needed.

He saw Bald Leggett run and jerk and run again. He began to stumble. Finally he slid face down in the snow where his massive body lay twitching, his outflung hands reaching toward the saloon building.

A bullet spat into the snow next to Matt, jarring him to the realization of his exposed position. He ducked behind a white fir seedling that struggled bravely in the open. In a moment he ducked out, working his way toward the fighting.

Parkis rode near and Matt waved him down. "How many left?"

"Some in that cabin we ain't burned.

245

Dill's in there."

Matt said, "Then give me your horse. Rest a while, Abe."

"Figured on resting," he said, dismounting. "It's Jud Keppel's turn to take over."

Matt mounted the tired horse and looked over the situation. Abe's crew was retiring, and Jud Keppel was leading his men out to replace them. That was good, Matt thought. Too many riders attacking a single cabin at once made too many targets. Matt spurred the horse toward the lone unfired cabin. Jud Keppel's men were working in, forming a tight circle.

Matt pulled alongside Keppel. "How many?"

"Seems like only one shooting," Jud Keppel said, in his odd high voice.

"Dill," Matt said hopefully. "Pull your men out, Jud. I want to go in."

This was the thing he had come for. He spurred to the rear of the shack so that he could dismount against the protection of a solid wall. Leaving the saddle, he checked his gun load and then walked around the small building. He moved steadily, his body thrown forward a little, his knees slightly bent for spring and balance. The heat made the snow slushy and the footing bad, but he walked on, rounding the corner, ducking under the shot-out window, and coming up against the closed door.

"Come out, Jake," he called.

"I ain't moving," Dill answered. "Come and take me, Ross."

"All right," Matt agreed quietly. He put out a hand, flipped the door latch, and plunged into the room.

Through smoke haze that hung in gray-blue layers, he could see Jake Dill. He stood with his back to the side wall, breathing hard through his mouth. Blood was running redly down the front of his shirt and down both sleeves onto the floor. He needed a shave worse than usual, and his grin was crooked through the whisker stubble. He had a gun in his hand, but it was pointed downward. He made a final effort to raise the gun toward Matt. The muzzle wavered, and the bullet plucked at Matt's hatbrim.

"Sometimes a man is too brave for his own good," Matt said to Dill. Deliberately, he shot Dill's gun away.

The gun slid across the dirt floor. Jake Dill fell, following it, the tips of his fingers reaching out and coming within a scant inch of the gun butt. He lay without moving. After a moment, Matt turned and walked out.

Chapter Fifteen

Back in town, the men took care of their wounded and then broke up to go to their homes. Matt, with Abe Parkis and Bede, walked toward the newspaper office.

"Now what?" Bede demanded.

"That," Matt said, pointing toward Lamont's saloon. Noise was boiling out from it much as it had on the night Jake Dill attacked Adam's newspaper.

"Evidently what we did at Shackville ain't going to quiet them," Abe Parkis said. He spat into the street. "And it ain't because they haven't heard of Shackville."

"Cole is still testing," Matt said. "He was counting on Jake, and now Jake is gone. He's trying to test me now through Lamont."

Adam nodded agreement. "It's what you've done that's making Pitman crawl," he told Matt. "He wants power, and you've forced him to go after it or quit. But once he starts himself — once he stops using others and uses his own men — he won't be as easy to stop as Dill was."

"So I know," Matt said. He listened to the noise from the saloons. Hewitt's was fairly quiet, but from Lamont's gunfire came, and the sound echoed through the streets. A burst of laughter whooped into the night, followed by another gunshot.

"Pitman has nothing left but his own power," Matt said. "Ezra hasn't much force — and I don't believe Lamont has. When Lamont is done, Pitman'll have to come against us with his own men. Are you ready for that, Abe?"

"I'm ready. We're all ready," Abe said.

"All right," Matt said, and started walking toward Lamont's.

As he stepped in, he saw that the place was far from full, but there were enough men to account for the noise. Two of Pitman's riders were at the bar, obviously drunk and looking for trouble. The shooting, Matt noticed, was aimed at a swamper. A bent, tired old man, he was being forced to dance in the center of the floor or else take a chance that the bullets aimed at the floor by his feet would hit him. He continued a painful shuffle even after Matt entered.

Lamont came forward from behind the bar as Matt headed his way. "Run out," he said testily.

Matt answered quietly, "There's no more Shackville, Lamont. No more Jake Dill. I'm still the law."

Lamont rocked on his toes, his handsome

features thoughtful. "As you were before?"

"As always," Matt said. "The law ordered no fighting drunks. Get rid of those two."

"I don't like your law," Lamont answered, and turned his back on Matt.

He made a show of serving the two loud-talking Pitman riders a drink. They were deliberately ignoring Matt, focusing their attention instead on the shuffling old swamper. But the others in the saloon ceased what they were doing and moved forward, the better to see how this challenge would be answered.

Matt said to the old man, "You can take a rest now," and stepped to the bar.

With a quick motion of his hand he knocked the liquor from the bar in front of the two men. He turned as they came for him, their guns lifted for slashing. He knocked their arms away and got his big fingers around the neck of each. The sound of their heads coming together was like that of a ripe pumpkin dropping to the ground.

Lamont watched the two men slide soggily to the floor. A soft surprised sigh went around the room. The old swamper had fallen to his knees, breathing painfully and noisily. Lamont continued to stare at Matt.

"A warning," Matt said. "Once more, and I close you up. See that these men ride for home before I get back." He walked out and continued on his regular rounds. When he returned the men were gone, and Lamont's was almost empty. Wearily, Matt left his work and went home to bed.

There was no more trouble in the next few days, but on Friday Adam Bede's paper appeared, almost daring Pitman to come out in the open.

Reading it at Gail's, Matt said, "There'll be no more quiet Fridays now that Adam prints this paper." He had finished his supper and was starting for the door. "And," he added, "I hear that Cole is mended and back in town."

Gail's kiss was brief but meaningful. Putting on his hat, Matt stepped into the night. The cold had finally broken, and a warm thin rain held promise of spring with its melting snows and mud-filled trails. It was a pleasant prospect only because summer and warmth lay ahead.

Matt was looking for Toby, and he found him at Daisy's talking to Jud Keppel. Matt looked Jud over. "You're getting fat," he observed. "Is Pitman beef that good at this time of year?"

"I've retired," Jud said leisurely. "When the mud goes I got a job for my crew to

251

help Jeremy Cotter move ore out of the mines. Until then, I'm retired."

"Don't retire too far," Daisy said, coming up. "Cole Pitman and some of his crew went into Lamont's not long ago."

Matt turned to Toby. "Watch close tonight. Nothing is finished yet."

Toby's nod was brief and distant. He had reluctantly returned to his duties since there was no longer any fear of tangling with Jake. But, Matt realized, since the sheriff had helped kill Jake, Toby didn't quite know how to act. The affection he had had for his father was a tenuous thing, and yet it had meant something to the boy. He could not break free all at once, nor did Matt expect him to.

Matt went into the night again. He walked slowly, enjoying the warm rain on his face, whenever he looked up at the lowering sky, and wondering how long the quiet that lay over the town would last.

About nine o'clock he heard a brief burst of noise from Lamont's, but it only lasted a moment and then died. Seeing Toby down in that direction, he went to his office to rest for a few moments. Toby came in shortly, to announce that all was going well, and then went out again.

By ten thirty Matt was beginning to doubt

that his ideas had been right. There was little noise anywhere, and only a few strollers were on the streets. He got up and started to find Toby, to tell him to go home and that he could finish this night alone.

He was still north of Hill when the batwing doors of Lamont's flew open, and a man staggered into the street to fall face down in the churned mud. The man picked himself up slowly and started for Matt in a weaving walk.

At first Matt thought it was a drunk, and then he recognized Toby Dill. Hurrying forward, he caught the boy as he stumbled on the boardwalk at the corner of Main and Hill. Matt drew him across the street where the light from the hotel lobby could fall on him. Even with the mud and grime on Toby's face, Matt could see that his lips and eyes were puffed. Blood dripped from his nose and from two cuts running down his cheeks.

"Pitman," Toby said painfully. "He and some of his men are getting liquored. Three of them ganged up on a Morgan man and threw him into the alley. I tried to stop them."

"Lamont gave you this beating?"

"Pitman," Toby said. "His men held me, and he did it."

"Gun whipped," Matt said, looking at the long cuts on Toby's face.

"Gun whipped," Toby agreed. He sounded as if he might cry.

Gently, Matt helped him to Adam Bede's and rapped on the door. Matt realized that this was the beginning of Pitman's challenge. He was making little noise about it, but it was the start.

Bede came to the door. Matt turned Toby over to him and then walked down to Lamont's. When he went in, Pitman and a few drunken hands were standing at the near end of the bar. Lamont was pouring out drinks for them, though the men were hard put to stand up without support. Texas Zinker smoked and drank alone a few feet away. The room was half filled.

"You're under arrest, Lamont," Matt said in a clear carrying voice. "This place is closed up. Everybody out."

Bill Lamont moved back a little. "That isn't good for business, Matt."

"It is for my business," Matt said levelly. "You, Cole, take your men and ride out of town." He knew that if he could force Pitman out he would gain more than by putting him in jail or giving him the gun whipping he had given to Toby. This and the closing of Lamont's would be the final nails in the coffin holding Pitman's self-respect.

Pitman showed no signs of his beating. He smiled without meaning. "You're going to run me out, Matt — from here?"

"Now," Matt said, and walked forward.

Pitman drew his gun and stood with his legs spread wide, waiting.

Matt kept on walking, his hands swinging free at his sides. Texas Zinker moved closer to Pitman. Matt said, "They'll string you up, Cole. Half the town will string you up and spit on your swinging carcass. They have no use for a degrader of women here. Put up your gun and get out."

Pitman's gun came up toward Matt's midriff. For all of his self-control, the effect of Matt's words showed in the anger twisting his features. White-lipped, he steadied the gun to make his shot.

"Not yet," Texas Zinker said softly. "Not yet, Captain."

Pitman hesitated, and then, slowly, the gun went back into his holster. "By God," he said hoarsely. "All right, Matt, I'll go — for now. I'll go and leave you to try and make the charges stick against Lamont."

"Take him out, Texas," Matt said.

"At my pleasure," Zinker answered, but he steered Pitman toward the door. Halting, he turned and beckoned to the Bar

Cross hands. They looked from Zinker to Matt and then, reluctantly, staggered outside into the rain.

"That was too easy," Lamont said mockingly.

"As easy as this," Matt agreed. "Come along, Lamont. You're out of business for the time being."

"Not tonight. I'll close up, but I won't come with you."

Matt walked to the bar and went around it, straight to Lamont. When he was close enough, he drew his gun and swung it. Lamont took the barrel on the jaw, staggered back, and buckled at the knees, incredulity mixed with the redness of blood on his face. Matt caught him as he fell.

"Get out," Matt said to the watching men. "This place is closed."

He carried and dragged Lamont to the street. Adam Bede and Abe Parkis stood there. Bede carried a shotgun in his hands.

"Pitman rode," Parkis said. He turned to some loiterers. "Give him a hand, boys."

When Lamont was safely in a cell, Matt said, "Toby?"

"I cleaned him and got him to your place," Adam Bede said. "Gail went to watch him. He'll be all right."

Leaving Abe Parkis to watch at the jail,

Matt and Adam Bede returned to Lamont's, where Bede witnessed the padlocking of the saloon. That done, Matt made a last check of Hewitt's, which was quiet, and then went home. He thanked Gail for her help, saw her to her door, and returned to bed.

He was awakened shortly after daylight by Adam Bede's pounding on his door. "The birds have flown," Bede said, when Matt let him in. "Pitman rode a crew into town and held a gun on Abe's belly while they pulled the bars from the cell window."

Matt wondered if his taste of success had made him underestimate Cole Pitman. "Why didn't you wake me?" he demanded.

"To chase them through the dark? They'll be back."

Matt thought, If he comes back that determined. . . . He said, "What about Gail?"

"Abe, having nothing left to guard, went to Gail's and took her home to his wife." In a moment, Adam Bede added, "We decided she'd better not be left alone after this."

"I'll see that she isn't," Matt agreed.

He dressed quickly, not bothering to shave, and went into the street. He was not surprised to see activity at Lamont's saloon. There would be little point in Lamont going free unless he openly flaunted that freedom in Gaptown.

Going to the saloon, Matt pushed his way past a pair of swampers into the dim main room and walked on up the stairs to Lamont's office. At his knock, Lamont called, "Come in," and, when he saw Matt, he said, "I expected this."

His face was bandaged. He sat behind his desk, his hands idly smoothing an unlighted cigar. Four of Pitman's hands lounged nearby.

Matt said, "You're under arrest. You and all of Pitman's crew."

Lamont shook his head. "You caught me short last night. It won't happen again."

This was the big challenge, Matt realized. If he failed this time he would be canceling all of his previous work. Because this was not just Lamont talking; he was Pitman's mouthpiece. He was the tenpin Pitman set up and dared Matt to knock down.

Matt said, "You'll be in jail by nightfall." He walked out and was nearly to the bottom of the stairs when Lamont called to him.

"Don't come back in here, Sheriff. I don't recognize your brand of law. You come back, and I'll shoot you for trespassing."

■ ■ ■ ■

Matt got his sorrel from the livery and rode for Morgan's Double M. The rain of the night before had ceased, though the clouds still hung low. The trails that had been ice-covered were now beginning to turn muddy, and it was labor for the horse to pull some of the steeper places. On the rise where the Double M sat, the snow had not all gone, but it was soft and slushy under the sorrel's hoofs.

Matt went to the rear door as he had in the past. Dave Morgan appeared, yawning and rubbing sleep from his eyes. He grinned at Matt and opened the door.

"Been raiding, Dave?"

"Trailing stock," Dave Morgan answered easily. "Come in, Matt. There's coffee on the stove."

"Trailing stock should be easy in the snow and mud," Matt answered. He went in and stood with his back to the stove. "Lots of sign over east?"

Morgan looked at the star on Matt's vest. "Pitman wasn't in, so we didn't stop to call," he said. He poured two cups of bitter-looking coffee, set the canned milk beside them, and sat down.

259

"He was in town — breaking open the jail," Matt said.

Morgan poured milk in his coffee and stirred slowly. "So?"

"I came for your help," Matt said flatly. It was a thing that hurt to say, but there was no other way. "It doesn't mean you're obliged. I'm asking." He lit a cigarette, sucking the smoke in deeply.

"I've been expecting Pitman to hit me here," Morgan said. "He has no place else to show his power."

"He has now," Matt said. "I think he plans to deal with you after the town is out of the way. We've challenged him openly." He explained what had taken place the night before. "When I put Lamont back in jail, Cole Pitman will try to prove himself to Gaptown. He'll have to — or what he does against you won't matter. He knows that if he doesn't beat us I'll jail him and all of his men as fast as I can. As soon as he finds out that Lamont and the four men he left with him are locked up, there's only one thing he can do — hit me."

"You want help guarding the jail?"

"After I get help putting Lamont behind bars." He looked down at his hands. "Those in town could do it. But it's your community, too, Dave, and I thought ——"

"Do we go as deputies?"

Matt understood what was behind the question. He said, "Yes, and let's say as citizens, too. Once it's over the law will hold on you as well as on the next man."

"We want no favors," Morgan said. "Only an equal chance." He finished his coffee. "I'll ask the men. They have a right to know what they're up against." Getting up, he started for the door. "I sent Lucy to town, thinking it was safer. Now I don't know."

"We'll send her back," Matt said. "And tell the men that Pitman will have the stronger force. His men know guns and fighting; it's their business."

When Morgan returned, he had four men and Pat Ryan, not counting the two who were left to guard the ranch. They rode to town as quickly as the road permitted and stopped by the old Chinese laundry. Matt sent two men through the alley to the rear of Lamont's, put two in front, and took Morgan and Pat Ryan with him into the saloon.

Once again Matt rapped at the door of Lamont's office, this time standing to one side and reaching out to hammer with the butt of his gun.

Lamont said, "I told you to keep out, Ross," and sent a bullet ripping through the

261

wooden panel of the door.

"You're surrounded," Matt said. "Come out peaceable or dead."

Another bullet, chest high, was the answer. Matt looked at Morgan and Pat Ryan beside him and got their nods. "All right," he said.

Three guns sent lead smashing into the door. Noise reverberated brashly through the saloon, and the stench of smoke grew strong as Matt and the Double M men emptied their forty-fours. They stopped to reload. Inside it was silent.

From the alley came a single shot, followed by the tinkling of glass. A man inside the office swore. Matt called, "I told you you were surrounded. Come out, Lamont."

They came slowly through the shattered door, Lamont first, with his hands high, and the four Pitman men behind him. As they passed, Pat Ryan relieved them of their guns and took knives from two as well. Matt herded them out, up the boardwalk through a small crowd of curious onlookers, past Meecham's just-opened bank, and into jail.

"Cole will hear of this," Lamont said. He seemed fully at ease.

"I hope so," was Matt's answer. He put Lamont in one cell and the four men in another. The center cell, which had been occupied the previous night, remained with an open hole gaping dismally where the window bars had been.

Morgan surveyed the scene. "We'll look things over, Matt. A good defender should know where his strength is."

Matt left him and went to eat. He found Adam Bede chuckling in Daisy's. "Ezra just rode out," Bede said. "Team and buckboard, hell-bent for the south."

"To tell Cole," Matt said. "Ezra will screech and holler so much Cole will have to fight to shut him up."

By early afternoon a delegation had gathered in Matt's office. The townsmen on the council were there except Ezra Meecham. Sam Garton acted as spokesman.

"You're making a battleground out of the town, Matt. If Pitman wins, he'll tear down the place and rebuild it to suit himself."

"It's your community," Matt said. "If you want I'll turn the men loose."

"No," Garton said, "we just wanted you to know we can do some shooting, too."

Matt smiled wryly at the joke. "I'll need every man," he said.

When they had gone, Morgan told Matt, "We're all set. Go get some rest. He won't hit until dark."

Agreeing, Matt went to his house. He

found Gail and Lucy there. Gail came to him as he entered, worry lines smoothing from her face. She took his hands and held them tightly.

"It's moving along," he told her. "Like a tree toppling. It's going, and we can't stop it."

Lucy came up. "How is Adam?"

"All right," Matt said. "So is Dave."

She flushed. "I know that Dave can take care of himself."

Matt was glad that she had brought up the subject. "Adam is very important, Lucy?"

Warm color ran up her neck and cheeks. "Very."

This, Matt knew, had started during his convalescence. Now it would come in handy to his plans. "Then," he said, "get him to take you and Gail to the ranch — and keep him there."

"He'll want to help," Lucy said.

"He can help by being away from here," Matt said. "Cole hates Adam and Gail as much or more than he hates me. I'm a symbol of law, and he'll destroy me if he can. Dave is in his way, and Cole will push him — if he can. But Adam and Gail are the voices and the scourge. I think Cole would destroy himself to get them."

Lucy's nod was understanding. "I'll try."

Matt thanked her with a nod. To Gail, he said, "Where is Toby? He didn't show up all day."

"He left hours ago," she answered. "He said he'd tell you that he was riding on."

Matt was silent a moment. "He's bitter at Cole for beating him up, and bitter at me for helping kill Jake. It can't be helped. I ____"

"You can talk later," Gail said. "Now it's time to rest."

Matt lay on the couch and listened to Gail's quiet movements about the house and to Lucy's slow rocking. After a while he drifted off to sleep. When he awoke, dusk was filtering through the windows and the smell of cooking came from the kitchen. A lighted lamp was on the parlor table, and he could see that Lucy's chair was empty.

Rousing himself, he found Gail in the kitchen. "You didn't go?"

"They didn't need a chaperone."

He felt a rush of annoyance. "Adam did take Lucy?"

"Some time ago."

"I wanted you to go," he said, "because Cole will try to destroy you."

"It's too late now," she answered. "Your supper is ready. You haven't much time.

265

Come and eat."

He knew her too well to argue. Besides, despite the strength of his idea that she should have gone, he saw how impossible it would be to get her away now. Washing, he sat to his meal, eating hurriedly. When he had finished, he went into the parlor. Gail came from the bedroom; Matt stared at her in amazement.

She wore a pair of his butternut jeans cut down to fit, an old flannel shirt, and heavy work boots. A man's flat-brimmed hat was over her rich piled hair, and she came toward him busily buckling a gun belt around her waist. The thirty-eight Matt had given her was in the holster.

"I haven't been idle this afternoon," she said. Taking a cowhide vest from a chair, she slipped it on. She saw his look. "Let me have my chance, too, Matt. Ellen was my cousin."

"It's no work for a woman," he said severely.

"Is blood on my hands worse than on yours?" she demanded.

Matt studied her for some time. Finally, he said, "There's a light rifle in the closet, Gail."

"I found it," she said, and pointed to where it stood by the front door. "And I've arranged with Luther for a horse, if I need one. Now I'll go to Main Street with you."

Matt bent and blew out the lamp. The only light left was from the banked fire flickering through the isinglass of the stove front. Both moved to the door but neither reached for the latch. Matt felt her move against him and he put out his arm, drawing her to his side. The brim of her hat struck him across the forehead. She laughed softly and tilted her head back, lying a little relaxed in his arms so that he had to search to find her lips.

"Now we can go," she said quietly.

Matt did not question Gail when she left him at the jail, went across the street, and disappeared into the livery. Shortly, she came out, riding a stocky pinto mare, and went down the street southward. She rode well, Matt noted, sitting her saddle as if she had lived a long while on the range. Matt went into his office, wishing she would ride toward Morgan's but holding little hope that she would do so.

Finding Morgan and his men resting comfortably, he went across the street to the livery stable. Luther Colban was in his haymow, settling himself down. The stablehand was at his side, cleaning a gun barrel.

"Some night," Colban observed. "Those clouds mean a dirty wet snow."

Matt went on to Garton's. He found Sam and his small crew of freight handlers rolling thick kegs and wooden boxes against the doors and windows. Satisfied, Matt retraced his steps and went into Abe's store. The shelves and bins were empty. There was only Abe Parkis there, sitting on his counter and squinting down the barrel of his old Henry rifle.

"Out of business, Abe?" Matt could see into the office and there was nothing there, not even the desk.

"Sam's men put my things in the same place they put Adam's press." His rusty chuckle came out gleefully. "It's all stored in Ezra Meecham's house. It'll be the last place they try to burn — if they get that far. We'll pay him rent for the time we use it."

"Good," Matt said. "Seen Toby?"

"He rode straight south this afternoon," Abe Parkis answered.

Matt returned to the street. It was dark now, with no hint of a moon or stars, and a heavy blanket of soggy cloud was lowering itself over the gap. Before Matt could get to the jail office, the first wet snowflakes slid from the sky and spattered on the boardwalk, melting almost as they touched.

268

Morgan was frowning when Matt went into the office. "Pitman could sneak in through a heavy snow."

Matt glanced out the window. While he watched, the fall began in earnest, heavy enough to blot out all but the vague outlines of the buildings across the street.

Chapter Sixteen

When Toby rode from town, he headed straight south. He had no destination in mind. His plan was simply to ride and let the air work on the bruises of his body and his mind.

Two things drove him. Matt had helped shoot Jake. That was Matt's job, but Jake had been his father, and that was something, too. He shook his head. This was getting him no place; it just kept his mind sore and touchy. He thought of the other thing. Cole Pitman had worked him over because he was doing his duty as the law. With no right at all a man had worked him over in public, when he was helpless to resist.

"Am I Matt's man or Jake's?" he asked himself. If he was Matt's, he would ride back and take his chances with the rest of them, understanding that Matt had gone after Jake because it was the only thing to do. But if he was Jake's man, as he had been raised, he would ride to the bench and shoot Cole Pitman before going on.

The idea of shooting rubbed him wrong. Too much Matt lately, he guessed. Still, the urge to move against Cole Pitman was strong, so strong that he could feel the pleasant bitterness of the desire to kill running through him. Before he made a conscious decision, he had turned up the path that led to the east bench.

He followed the trail until he could see Pitman's house in the near distance. Then it came to him that he could be ambushed easily. A guard might think he was sent by Matt and might draw on him before he got an explanation out. Sudden fear made him give the horse its head, and when he had calmed enough to rein in he found himself on the familiar trail to the mines. Toby carefully turned the horse back to Pitman's trail.

A cold wind came up from the south. It chilled him, making him aware that winter wasn't really yet over. But he pressed on, hunched into his coat. Only one thing was in his mind — if he shot Cole Pitman he would feel better, lighter inside.

He rode openly toward the Bar Cross, realizing that it was the safest attitude. Reaching it, he reined in before the veranda and waited. He tried to look insolent, sitting there as if it were summer. The cold bench breeze flapped at the brim of his hat and pinched his thin nostrils.

Texas Zinker opened the door. "Come in out of the cold, Dill."

"It's Pitman I want," Toby answered. The darkness of his eyes stood out in his thin face. "That's all."

"You won't get far shooting the captain," Zinker told him. He smiled down at Toby, shaking his head. Then he whistled sharply. A noise made Toby look toward the top of the house. A dormer window in the upper half story opened, and a man with a rifle leaned out.

Toby licked his lips and forced a laugh. "Tell him to shut the window," he said to Zinker. "It's too cold to be out in the open." He got off his horse and walked into the house, keeping his hands carefully away from his sides. Zinker took his gun as he walked past. In a way, Toby was relieved. Now there was no need to make a decision about shooting Pitman.

Pitman was in a chair in the parlor when Toby came in. Toby took a stand with his back to the fireplace, shivering a little. "You should have lain on the trail and waited for me," Pitman gibed.

"Too cold," Toby complained. "Seems like every place is too cold right now."

"Was this the sheriff's idea?" When Toby shook his head, Pitman added, "Fifty a month isn't much to pay a man for killing, is it?"

Toby stared woodenly at him. Feeling somewhat thawed, he took out a sack of tobacco and rolled a cigarette. Lighting it, he tossed the match into the fire behind him. Then he crossed to a nearby chair and sat down.

"What happens to me now?"

"Tie a can to your tail and send you back to town."

"Go slow, Captain," Zinker warned.

Something in his voice made Pitman turn and stare at him. Together they left the room. Toby stayed, smoking his cigarette and wishing he had made his break good the night Matt had caught him at Abe Parkis' store.

Cole Pitman came back alone. "Take a nap, kid. Use the sofa there." He relaxed, smoking his cigar as if he had no cares, no problems.

Toby stared out the window and watched a wrangler take his horse around to the barn. He looked back at Pitman but received no sign of recognition. When he realized no one was going to talk to him or do anything to him, he stretched out on the sofa and tried to sleep. He was there when Ezra Meecham came screeching up in his buckboard. Toby lay perfectly still, though he was wide awake.

Meecham started in immediately. Cole Pitman cut him off short. "I heard," he said. "One of Lamont's men rode in ahead of you."

"We're ruined," Meecham squawled. "Men won't come to a town with laws like Ross's. And you still hold Lamont's note. You stand to lose if he's shut up for good." Pitman failed to look impressed, and he added, "But that's nothing to the way the town'll treat you if Ross gets away with this."

"You don't have to tell me that," Pitman said angrily. "Tell Texas."

Zinker, who had come in on Meecham's arrival, said, "It's time. They won't let you wait until winter's over. Now's the time." He lapsed back into silence.

Pitman rubbed his chin a moment. Then he said, "Texas, go show Ezra where he can rest." When they had gone, he turned to Toby. "You can come awake, Dill. We'll ride tonight, and this is the end of Ross's law. It's the end of Ross or of me — and I don't figure it to be me. You can ride with us or go down with the town."

"Let a man sleep," Toby said.

"Now," Pitman went on, "if someone like you were to ride back with a story about how you saw our riders splitting — some going for the Double M, some going for town ——"

Toby said nothing.

Pitman smiled. "It's worth two hundred gold, Toby, and maybe a job as sheriff when things quiet down."

Toby lay there, thinking, wondering if there was some way he could get to town and warn Matt that Pitman was riding. But the risk seemed too great. There was too much Jake in him, he thought. He fell asleep thinking about it.

Pitman woke him to eat supper. Afterward, he put it up to Toby again. Toby said, "All right, Pitman."

Pitman nodded in seeming satisfaction. "And maybe the sheriff's job," he said. "That was to be Jake's — only he never got the chance."

Again Toby felt unreasoning bitterness toward Matt. He looked outside at the growing dusk. "I'll go now," he said.

Pitman called to Zinker, who brought Toby his gun and a hundred dollars in gold eagles. The gun was empty, and Zinker dropped the cartridges in Toby's pocket. "Your horse is out back," he said.

"What if you lose?" Toby asked Pitman.

"We don't lose," Pitman said. "Not this round. We've got too much strength. I've had men coming in all day to tell me what the town is up to."

Toby understood what he meant — this was like the war. Only now Pitman was the general, not just a captain. He would have his strategy all figured out. Toby wished he could get the information from him.

Texas Zinker said, "If we lose you lose, too. Give your message and lay low."

Toby went silently through the kitchen and outside. Mounting, he rode through the thickening dark to the valley. He paused there, at the forks. The bullets in his coat pocket felt heavy, and he put them back into his gun. The gold was heavy, too, but only half as heavy as it could be. He spent a moment feeling it. Damn a man who played it so close, he thought. Two hundred gold was a lot of money.

It was full dark now, and Toby could see the glow of Gaptown lights off to the north. It began to snow — thick wet flakes that spattered on his face and, finally, shut out the distant lights. Not a good night to be out, Toby thought, but he reckoned that he could stand it for a time. He had a full belly and a stake in his pocket, and it wasn't too long a ride to Lewiston. Laughing softly, he pulled the horse to his left and rode south.

"Not enough Jake in me," he said to the horse.

Matt could see nothing. He could hear hoofbeats, and he waited in the jailhouse to parley with Pitman when he came. The hoofbeats faded and then rose again, coming from the south and the east. Matt looked across at Dave Morgan, questioning in his eyes. At that moment gunfire rippled through the sullen snow-filled night.

"Parley, hell," Morgan scoffed. "They're hitting at the start."

"I give a man too much credit," Matt said, and looked to his gun.

A rider appeared, dim through the snow. Then another followed, and another. They circled, coming from two directions, crossing each other's paths and then disappearing. That meant they were trying to draw fire so that all the defenders might be located. Matt waited until a rider came into his sights, and he fired. The man looped into the air, a dim shadow in the snow, and whirled out of sight. The horse bolted up the street.

As if Matt's shot had been a signal, men fired from their vantage points at Colban's, at Garton's, and from Abe's. The circling stopped, and there was a heavy silence.

"They've spotted our positions," Matt said.

Firing broke out again, suddenly, filling the gap with its echoes. Matt caught it from the cells behind them, from across Main Street, from down toward Abe's place. Pitman's men would be hard to box now that they knew what to watch for. There was answering fire from across Main; then it broke off, and a shout went up. Matt recognized it as Luther Colban's bellow. The reason was evident — Abe Parkis' had been fired.

Matt turned. "Hold this place," he ordered Dave Morgan. He plunged out into the snow, moving rapidly through shadow toward the fire-lighted corner. He could see two forms lying in the snow of the street as he crouched back into the recess of Adam Bede's doorway. Riders appeared again, seeping through the snow, swirling down the street, and drawing fire from both sides of Main. One man went down as his horse slipped and threw him. Clambering to his feet, he started to weave toward the corner by the bank. Someone from the jail office got him in their sights and fired. He pitched and jerked and went headlong. He made the corner but his feet stayed on Main, showing for a moment before snow covered them.

Matt saw the reason for this apparently senseless attack. The shop where he crouched began to flame. Pitman was holding everyone's fire to Main while his men worked their way to the buildings and set them alight.

Matt broke away from his hiding place, realizing the futility of it as flames shot light all along Main Street. He cut toward the alley. Sounds of shooting from the rear of the jail were steady now. Matt ducked into shadow and sought for a man, any man.

The anger in him was pounding like a boiler filled with steam. He was tense, trying to probe the fire-lighted snow-filled night. The flames at Bede's flared violently, throwing a bright glow into the alley. Matt was ready as five men charged down — but the light showed Dave Morgan and his crew, and he pulled back. They were panting, running and sliding through the snow. A rider came behind him, firing and making a poor job of it as his horse kept slipping.

Matt took aim and shot. The rider swung in the saddle, and Matt shot again. This time the man left his horse and landed in the snow, where he lay jerking crazily. Matt jumped after the running men, following them back across Main Street to the temporary safety of Ira Morris' empty hardware store. Dave Morgan met him with a sour look.

"They broke into the jail," he panted. "We couldn't hold it against two dozen." Before he finished speaking, smoke rolled from the office across the street and fire hissed at the falling snow. "They're soaking with coal oil," he added. "Look at her burn!"

"The whole town will go up," Matt said bitterly. "We should have figured out what Cole would do. He'll hit for your ranch next."

Morgan said, "We can't hold anything here — there isn't much left to hold. I want to ride for home."

The realization that Pitman had out-generaled him so easily was painful to Matt. He could only agree with Dave Morgan. "See if you can get to your horses," he said.

He watched them break for the rear of the livery, Morgan and Pat Ryan covering their men. There was a sudden burst of gunfire as a small group of riders swept around the rear of the bank. But now Colban and Garton were covering from their spots, and all the Double M men made it safely. The Pitman riders split under the driving lead, melting back into the obscurity of snow and shadow.

Matt worked his way along the alley, his eyes searching every shadow, every movement. He slipped across Main, down near the south end, and went up past Hewitt's. He went cautiously, staying in shadow. The town was about gone, but Pitman remained. That was his goal now — to find Cole Pitman. To do that he had to stay alive, and so he was as cautious as possible.

But they seemed to have disappeared. Pitman and Pitman's men. Matt noted that the jail had been opened and Lamont, with the four Bar Cross men, had flown. Over on State nothing seemed touched. Now and then shooting would come from Main, but by the time Matt worked his way there no one was in sight. Time passed — how much Matt could not judge. Then a round of solid firing drew him again to Main, and he was in time to see riders passing Garton's and rounding the corner there. Matt hastened to the alley west of Main, but there was no sign of life. It stretched blankly southward, dimmed by the falling snow.

From the shooting, Matt gathered that Colban and Garton were still holding out.

He wondered if Abe had got free before his store went up, and he wondered, too, about Jud Keppel. Where was he at a time like this?

Matt had reached the bank when the sound of hoofbeats came from the south end of Main. He lifted his gun and waited, peering through the snow toward the riders. They crossed Hill, kept northward on Main, and thundered past his position. He was about to fire when shooting flame from the last of Abe Parkis' store threw the night into harsh brightness.

Matt whispered, "You crazy fools!"

One of the riders was Adam Bede — there was no mistaking that flamboyant figure. The other was Gail. She rode without a hat, her hair streaming behind her, so that she was unmistakably identified.

It took Matt but brief seconds to realize what had happened. Gail, knowing Pitman's hatred for herself and Bede, had gone to the Double M for him. Now they were riding together to draw away Pitman. And, Matt saw, she had not been wrong. Shortly after she and Bede swept by the corner of Hill a group of riders rounded it, Pitman leading. His voice rose in a senseless bellow. Matt could see Zinker beside him, and even above the crackle of flames and the pounding of hoofs, Zinker's voice was plain.

"Patience, Captain!"

But whatever patience Pitman had possessed and whatever restraint Zinker had had over him were gone. With most of his crew, he raced after Gail and Adam Bede.

Matt lifted his gun and fired. But Pitman's men had not lost all caution. They poured lead into every shadow, every possible hiding place for a defender, and they rode weaving from one side of the street to the other. In the driving snow they were almost impossible targets, and though their motions made their own shooting bad, the hail of lead drove Matt back to cover.

He stepped out again, firing futilely. Ahead he made out Gail and Bede rounding the far corner of Garton's. The men there and at Luther Colban's managed to knock off a pair of Pitman's riders, and then they, too, were out of sight.

Swearing, Matt ran stumblingly onto Main and up to the livery. He shouldered into the stable, throwing the big doors wide, and called out his name. Luther Colban and Abe Parkis, who had somehow managed to work his way from the store, tumbled down from the loft.

Colban said, "They didn't all go. Lamont and them in the jail ——"

Matt had located his sorrel saddled and

waiting in a stall. He drew the animal out and mounted. "Do what you can," he said harshly. "I'm going after them."

"Look —" Parkis began.

Matt interrupted. "Gail and Bede deliberately pulled them off the town. The least we can do is help." He sent the sorrel out the door and into the street, reining northward. The horse had a little trouble with his footing at first, but then they settled down to steady hard riding.

Matt knew what lay ahead. Gail and Bede would be breaking trail and so would be giving the advantage to Pitman and his crew. His own chance lay in that the sorrel was fresh while the others rode already tired mounts. He pressed on, following the now well broken trail down the freight highway. From behind he heard a few shots, which meant that some of Pitman's crew were still there fighting. Ahead he could see nothing. The snow had thinned, almost stopped, but the moon was thin and watery behind low scudding clouds, and the twists and turns in the freight road made seeing far impossible.

Once he heard a shot — otherwise there was only the pounding of the sorrel's hoofs to break the silence.

Topping a low rise, Matt had to slow the

sorrel on the downgrade to prevent it from slipping and falling. Now, ahead, he could hear the sounds of riders, and he knew that he was closing in on them. Suddenly, the trail broken in the snow left the highway, taking off abruptly toward the northern limits of Morgan's benchland. This would be the trail that Matt had used the day he met Lucy searching for stock and found Jud Keppel's canyon. The snow would lie deep up there, and he wondered how Gail and Bede could manage to push their tiring horses through it.

He turned the sorrel and followed, urging, leaning forward to throw his weight better, whispering words of encouragement to the slipping, staggering horse. Finally they topped the bench.

The moon came through the clouds more strongly, and Matt could see along the tree-dotted expanse of flat land. Almost within firing distance, he made out Pitman's men riding hard, streaming across the snow toward two distant dots that could only be Gail and Adam Bede.

As he rode, Matt worked bullets into his forty-four. Occasionally there was a shot from ahead, but the two in the lead managed somehow to stay safely in front. Yet even in the deceptive moonlight Matt could see the distances shortening. He was closing in on the tired Bar Cross horses, and they in turn were slowly but inevitably moving up on the riders in the lead.

With startling abruptness Gail and Adam Bede disappeared. It was not until Matt followed the tracks to his right that he realized the strategy. Gail and Bede were seeking refuge in Jud Keppel's canyon. Refuge and, Matt prayed, help.

There was no chance of concealment for them now. Pitman was too close. When Matt had located Gail and Bede again they were just ducking into the gap that led to the canyon. Pitman and his men were not two minutes behind, and Matt, close enough so that the drag rider of the Bar Cross turned and fired at him, pressed on without hesitation.

The thunder of hoofs was loud in the narrow gap, reverberating deafeningly from the sheer rock walls. It was short, Matt knew, yet the distance seemed endless; the time was like hours insteads of moments before he broke from the narrow passage into the barren cup of the valley.

Gail and Bede had almost reached the dark, silent mass of Keppel's shack. Now Pitman and his crew were firing, shooting with no regard for the fact that one of those ahead was a woman. Matt saw Bede jerk in the saddle, saw Gail stiffen as if she had been slapped, and then they were around the side of the building. Then sudden roaring fire burst from the windows, and guns cracked from the snow-covered hillside behind Matt.

He drew rein, jerking the sorrel out of the line of fire. The Bar Cross crew broke into a frantic milling. Three went down, and the others swirled to one side, clustering there out of range.

Now it was Matt's turn. Taking advantage of the bewilderment of Pitman and his men, he cut toward them. Low on his horse, he put the sorrel full tilt into the group. His forty-four opened up, and one man crashed to the snow. Lead pulled at his hat, and then he charged into the midst of the dozen or so men left in the saddle. He was seeking Cole Pitman. The anger in him had burst, and he had but one thought — Pitman.

Men were racing from Jud Keppel's cabin, and others were riding down from the hillside. The Bar Cross men milled, and Texas Zinker's voice could be heard striving to organize them. Then Matt was in their midst like the wind of fury. He was too close now to be shot at — they could not fire without taking the chance of hitting one of their own men. A rifle butt slashed out, clubbing his shoulder, half spinning him from the saddle. Almost automatically he fired and pressed on.

"Pitman!" He shouted his challenge and strove to see in the milling group of horses and men.

A rider came abreast of him, his horse shouldering roughly at the sorrel. Matt recognized the bearded face of Texas Zinker and saw his forty-four lifted and leveled. Matt, thrown out of position by the blow against his horse, twisted in the saddle and fought to bring up his own gun. He fired as he moved. Zinker's gun muzzle blossomed flame, and the lead slammed against Matt's side, twisting him still more in the saddle. He saw his own shot pluck at Zinker's hat, and he fired again. Zinker's face took on a look of immense surprise, his body rose and settled back, and he cascaded off to one side and fell in the snow. At that moment a hoard of riders, Keppel's men, shouting and clubbing, swarmed in. The last that Matt saw of Zinker, he was trying to crawl out from under the slashing, driving hoofs of the frantic horses. Matt heard his voice above the mass of sound.

"Now, Captain. Ride him down! Now is the time."

Matt thought, His patience has broken at last. Then, his side throbbing, he jerked the sorrel about. His shout rose again, "Pitman!"

He saw a rider break from the group, burst out onto the clear untrampled snow, and race toward the gap. The man's figure was unmistakable. It was Pitman. Matt swore and beat with his gun, freeing a path for himself, driving the sorrel out of the press, leaving the brawling to others. Pitman was almost to the gap, almost to safety.

The sorrel broke clear at last, staggering under Matt's frantic spurring. Matt could make out Pitman again just before the dark mouth of the gap closed around him. He pushed the sorrel up the slope and into the hole. The moonlight was abruptly cut off, and blackness closed around him. Ahead he could hear the beat of hoofs on the rock floor of the gap. Suddenly there was a heavy crash, and Pitman's swearing rose in the darkness.

"Damn you, Ross," he said. "I should have let Jake Dill stop you like he stopped your father."

Before Matt could do more than realize that at last he knew the truth of Tim Ross's death, his horse's forelegs struck something soft and yielding, and the sorrel fell. Matt pitched out of the saddle, landed shoulder down on Pitman's fallen mount, and rolled to his feet. The fall sent pain cascading upward from the wound in his side. He could feel the warm blood running down his hip and along his leg, filling his boot.

He stood motionless in the dark, his back pressed against the icy wall of the gap. Only the sobbing breathing of the two exhausted horses, both too spent to rise, came to his ears. There was no more indication that anyone else was with him.

Matt said, "Pitman!"

A gun flamed, and rock splinters chipped off by Matt's face. He freed his gun and fired at the flame. But Pitman had moved, and there was only the whine of his lead from the stone. He moved, too, as he fired, but Pitman's answering shot caught him in the thigh, throwing him hard against the cliff, driving the breath from his body with the impact of pain. The stench of burned powder was strong on the air, and the echo of gunshots roared in his ears. Matt felt himself falling and he staggered forward, pushing himself from the wall.

Pitman's gun roared again. The blast was not three feet away, but Matt's push threw him aside from the bullet. He turned as he fell, raising the gun that felt like a ton of weight in his hand. He did not go completely down but balanced himself on his knees while he sought Pitman in the dark. There was the slightest movement, and he pulled the trigger. He heard the sound of the bullet as it found Pitman, and then pain shut out everything else from him.

When he walked from the gap, the moonlight was bright in his eyes. He saw swirling forms below him, about Jud's cabin, but the shooting seemed to have stopped. He went that way slowly, dragging his wounded leg a little.

Adam Bede came to meet him. "All over," he said cheerfully. He looked more closely at Matt. "You're hit."

"Not bad," Matt said. They walked together to the shack and went inside. Two lighted lamps were turned up high, and in the lamplight Matt saw Gail. She still wore man's clothing, her hair hung loose and free, her face was smudged with dirt, and a thin line of blood coursed down her forehead. Behind her stood Jud Keppel and some of his men.

Matt said. "They're all gone?"

"All gone," Jud Keppel said in his odd voice.

Adam pointed toward a bunk. "I want to

see where you were hit."

Wearily, Matt obeyed. His side and his thigh ached, though neither wound was serious. He did not particularly want to be doctored, but he did want to rest.

When Matt was checked to Adam Bede's satisfaction, they all rode for town. It was a slow procession, and dull gray daylight had broken by the time they arrived. On the way Matt pieced out from the talk swirling around him that Pitman had sent part of his crew against the Double M when he rode on Gaptown. Old Pete, with Adam and Lucy, had kept them off until Dave and his men arrived. Jud Keppel had shown up about the same time, and together they had squeezed the Bar Cross attackers into nothing.

It was then that Adam Bede was free to follow Gail's plan, and, sending Jud back to his canyon, he had ridden back to Gail in town.

They were a silent group as they rode in. Main Street looked like a great holocaust had swept over it. All of the buildings on upper Main were only smoking ashes, but for Ezra's bank. Farther on they saw that even Bee's had been burned. And where Lamont's had stood, only a tall stone chimney remained.

Abe Parkis met them. He was limping a little, his face lined with weariness. "Come and eat," he said. "Daisy's set up shop in the parsonage."

Matt looked down the street. "Did they burn out Lamont, too?"

"We holed up them that stayed in there," Abe Parkis said rustily. "Then we did some burning. They didn't get out."

Jud Keppel's odd voice came from behind Matt. "Them up there didn't have much chance. Not after Matt rode into them like a danged Injun. I never saw nothing like it."

Abe said, "Pitman?"

It was Adam who answered. On their way through the gap he had stopped, dismounted, and lighted a match while he examined Cole Pitman. "One shot," he said. "Through the heart. Matt got him."

Matt suddenly felt very tired again, and he was glad when they reached the parsonage and went into Daisy's "restaurant." She was there as usual, smiling through her weariness, serving a scattering of townsmen who, still too keyed up to sleep, sat and drank coffee and talked over what had happened.

Someone remarked that Adam Bede was limping. He answered, laughing, "Only scratched me. A shot in the leg doesn't stop a man from setting type, anyway. I'll be back at it as soon as the press is up. Is there anyone here who hasn't subscribed to the *Gazette*?"

Abe Parkis made a chuckling sound. "I'd say Ezra'll let you print right in his house, Adam. He's feeling mighty cooperative about now. Even said he thought Gail'd make a good schoolteacher! Not that he could stop her, after everyone signed your petition."

Matt sought Gail and found her seated alone at one of the improvised tables, made of planks and sawhorses. He joined her.

"That was a crazy thing you did."

She answered softly, "Ellen was my cousin, Matt."

"Was that the only reason?"

"I've told you before that a woman should stand by her husband."

"First," Matt said, "the woman has to have a husband."

Gail's low laugh was warming to hear. "Adam and Jud and I think they should elect Abe Parkis justice of the peace. When they rebuild the town, Abe will be here as judge if you have anyone to arrest."

Matt said again, "Is that the only reason?"

"He can marry people, too," she said. She laughed again. "We think he should be elected tomorrow."

Matt laughed with her and, ignoring the others about him, he drew her face toward his. Her hair cascaded forward, hiding them both.

ABOUT THE AUTHOR

Stuart Brock is the *nom de plume* under which **Louis Trimble** wrote five exceptional Western novels, all published by Avalon Books in the 1950s. Trimble was born in Seattle, Washington, and during most of his professional career taught in the University of Washington system of higher education. 'I began writing Western fiction,' he later observed, 'because of my interest in the history and physical character of the western United States and because the Western was (and is) a genre in which a writer could move with a good deal of freedom.' His first Western novel under the Louis Trimble byline was *Valley of Violence* (1948). In this and his subsequent Western novels he seems to have been most influenced by Ernest Haycox, another author who lived in the Pacific Northwest. The point of focus in his Western fiction, whether he is writing as Louis Trimble or Stuart Brock, constantly shifts among various viewpoints and women are often major characters. *Railtown Sheriff* (1949) was Trimble's first Western novel as Stuart Brock and it was under this byline that some of his most exceptional work appeared, most notably *Action at Boundary Peak* and *Whispering Canyon,* both in 1955, and *Forbidden Range* in 1956. These novels have strong characters, complex and realistic situations truly reflecting American life on the frontier, and often there is a mystery element that heightens a reader's interest. The terrain of the physical settings in these stories is vividly evoked and is an essential ingredient in the narrative. Following his retirement from academic work, Trimble made his retirement home in Devon, England.

We hope you have enjoyed this Large Print book. Other Thorndike, Wheeler, Kennebec, and Chivers Press Large Print books are available at your library or directly from the publishers.

For information about current and upcoming titles, please call or write, without obligation, to:

Publisher
Thorndike Press
295 Kennedy Memorial Drive
Waterville, ME 04901
Tel. (800) 223-1244

or visit our Web site at:

http://gale.cengage.com/thorndike

OR

Chivers Large Print
published by BBC Audiobooks Ltd
St James House, The Square
Lower Bristol Road
Bath BA2 3SB
England
Tel. +44(0) 800 136919
email: bbcaudiobooks@bbc.co.uk
www.bbcaudiobooks.co.uk

All our Large Print titles are designed for easy reading, and all our books are made to last.

Due Date
8-12-19 EL

Carter
SAmariTan.
monor
Gloss